Art of Love

Pride, Oregon
Book 19

Jill Sanders

GRAYTON

This is a work of fiction. Names, characters, places, and incidents either are the product of the author's imagination or are used fictitiously, and any resemblance to actual persons, living or dead, business establishments, events, or locales is entirely coincidental.

DIGITAL ISBN:

Text copyright © 2025 Grayton Press

All rights reserved.

Copyeditor: Erica Ellis–inkdeepediting.com

No part of this book may be reproduced, scanned, or distributed in any printed or electronic form without permission. Please do not participate in or encourage piracy of copyrighted materials in violation of the author's rights. Purchase only authorized editions.

Summary

She's here to expose his past. He's here to escape it. But some secrets refuse to stay buried.

Dylan Beck never planned on coming back to Pride, let alone going undercover in her own hometown. As a private investigator, she's used to getting close to her targets without getting involved, but this case is different. She's been hired to dig into the past of Abe Collins, the chart-topping musician with a troubled history. Years ago, a car accident claimed the life of a young woman he was involved with—and now, someone wants to know if he had a role in it. Dylan is just here to do a job... not to fall for the man behind the music. But from the moment she hears his voice, her tough exterior starts to crack.

Abe Collins is looking for an escape. The pressure of fame is suffocating, and a summer at his friend Max's newly restored lighthouse promises the solitude he desperately needs. But when he crosses paths with a captivating stranger on the beach who doesn't seem fazed by his fame, he feels something stir deep inside him, something he thought had died along with Kara, the only woman he'd ever loved. Dylan is a challenge he can't resist, and breaking through her walls becomes his new obsession.

But neither of them realizes that someone will do anything to keep the past buried. What really caused the accident is more dangerous than they ever imagined, and as Dylan gets closer to uncovering the truth, the real culprit will stop at nothing to keep her from it.

To my Dad,
Losing you while writing this book was very difficult.
Your goofy storytelling and sense of humor live on—and will never be forgotten.

Dear reader,
If your parents are still with you, call them. Hug them.
Spend time with them.
Time is the real enemy.

Prologue

Ten-year-old Dylan itched to blurt out the answer to her teacher's riddle. But she'd already been scolded by Mrs. Pepper twice that morning in class and didn't want to chance another time. Instead, she waved her hand in the air and waited as her teacher called on four other students first.

"You're a clock!" she shouted when Mrs. Pepper finally called her name.

"Yes, Dylan, you are correct."

Mrs. Pepper didn't look pleased that she'd guessed correctly.

Dylan always guessed correctly. She couldn't help it that her brain solved puzzles better than anyone else's. Even her dad, who was a veterinarian, asked her for help when he was stumped by his word puzzles.

Today's riddle had been super easy, and she was surprised that none of the other kids got the answer right. Then again, most of the kids in her class were staring out the window, counting the seconds until recess or lunchtime, the one part of the school day that she hated, mainly because she spent those times alone. Up until last year, she'd spent that time with Lucy McDonald, her very best and only friend.

Lucy's home life had been bad.

She was the middle child out of three and the only girl. Her older brother, Tom, was a few years older than them in school and was somewhat of a bully. Kenny, her younger brother, was a grade below them and was pretty awesome.

Since Dylan was an only child, she often pretended that Kenny was her brother instead of Lucy's.

It was obvious, at least to Dylan, that Lucy's dad was abusive to his entire family, even Lucy. She'd never witnessed it firsthand, but there were signs, and everyone in town gossiped about it. Her mother, Emma, was always jumpy and apologizing for everything, and the kids were sometimes covered in bruises.

No kids were ever invited over to their trailer, and when Dylan asked if Lucy could come to her place, she'd been told no.

Then, a couple years ago, Mrs. McDonald had packed up the kids and moved into her mother's goat farm just outside of town.

A while after that, Mr. McDonald was arrested and Lucy was back at school full time. But she had changed. She had made friends with Jennifer and Stephanie, two of the most popular girls in their class, and Dylan had been left friendless again.

Dylan had gotten much luckier in the parent department. Well, her mother had died long before Dylan could even remember her, but her dad made up for her lack of a mother. He was the best person on the planet.

Whatever she had asked for, her dad had given it to her.

He was kind, patient, smart, and, to her ten-year-old mind, handsome enough to win any woman over.

But the longer it was just her and him, the clearer it became that no matter how much she wanted a new mom, none would come. Just like a new friend.

She glanced back at where Lucy was sitting, whispering and giggling with Jennifer, and felt her stomach drop when their eyes moved towards her and they burst out laughing again.

Maybe not having a mom to dress her in girlie clothes or braid her hair was one of the reasons she always got picked on. She was a tomboy through and through. She didn't even own a dress, let alone anything with flowers or rainbows on it, like Lucy and Jennifer were wearing.

Dylan's light brown hair was always like a mouse's nest, wild and often falling in her face. She usually had dirt under her fingernails and always had stains on her worn jeans.

She didn't own anything other than tennis shoes and didn't care for the sandals that most girls in her class were always wearing.

Besides, most of the time, Lucy and Jennifer talked about boys. She knew from the books that she read that it was far too early for girls their age to like boys, so she guessed that they were faking it to be popular.

She would never fake anything. It was stupid.

That afternoon, as she walked home, she wondered why the other kids avoided her. Why was Lucy not her friend any longer?

It couldn't be just the clothes. Could it?

Dylan had stuck by Lucy's side when she'd show up at school bruised, afraid, and behind in her homework. Dylan had helped her catch up. They'd spent recess time studying for the spelling test or math test Lucy hadn't known about because she'd missed school. Dylan had even let her copy some of her homework. Just the notebook stuff, nothing too much.

So what made Dylan Roselyn Beck so unlikeable? Whatever it was, she was determined to find out and fix it. After all, life was the biggest mystery there was to solve, and she knew that, whatever the answer was, she'd get to the bottom of it. Not by pretending to be someone she wasn't, but by being the best Dylan she could be.

In the end, it had taken Dylan a few years to find herself and decide who she would become. When she did, she no longer cared about making friends or being popular. Instead, she lived to find answers. To? Well, everything, of course.

Shortly after graduation, she moved out of her small hometown and only came back a handful of times in the next few years. She traveled all over the States and did what she loved—finding answers.

Chapter One

The last time Dylan had lived in her childhood home back in Pride, she'd had a freshly printed high school diploma and an associate's degree, thanks to all the college classes she'd taken online during high school. All of her worldly possessions were packed in the trunk of her old Subaru.

She'd left without looking back, heading straight to Portland, where she spent the next four years immersed in classes on criminal law, police investigations, and forensic psychology. She had loved every single moment of it. The structure, the challenges, the sense of purpose—it was everything she had craved growing up in a town that had always felt too small for her ambitions.

To fill the hours she wasn't studying, she started working for a small PI firm just outside of Portland. It hadn't taken long for her to realize she had a knack for the work. Digging into people's lives, uncovering secrets, piecing together puzzles—she had fallen in love with every bit of it. So, naturally, she'd started her own PI business after graduation. No boss. No limitations.

Now, two years later, her business was easily as busy as the last firm she'd worked for.

Which was how she found herself back in Pride at the beginning of the summer.

For the next two months, she was going to follow one of the nation's sexiest chart-topping music artists.

Kevin Sinclair, her client, had walked into her freshly painted, one-room office in downtown Portland and hired her to get to the bottom of an old family tragedy. She'd been excited about the case, then she'd heard the name of the man he suspected.

Abe Collins.

The Abe Collins. Music superstar of the decade. The man whose voice filled her apartment on rainy nights when she was feeling lonely. The one she danced to while making breakfast on weekends when she never left her loft apartment. The one whose songs had gotten her through some of the darkest moments of her life after her father's death last year.

That Abe Collins.

She'd had to work to keep her reaction neutral as Kevin slid a thick envelope across her desk. Inside were photos, schedules, and a neatly typed check with a figure that made her pulse skip. It was more money than she'd ever made on a single job.

Her PI license was valid in Oregon, Washington, and California, and she had assumed she would be heading to LA at first. After all, everyone knew that Abe lived on a horse ranch outside the city, tucked away in the hills where the press couldn't hound him.

But then she'd heard a rumor. One that placed him a whole lot closer to home.

So instead of hopping on a flight to California, she'd taken the two-hour drive south and ended up right back where she'd started. In Pride, Oregon. The one place she had spent the last year trying to avoid.

The last time she had been here, it had been to bury her father and lock up the property she'd grown up in and had inherited.

Now, as she pulled into her small hometown, she wasn't sure what unsettled her more—being back in a place she had sworn she'd never return to or that her first big case involved shadowing a man she had spent years obsessing over.

Either way, she figured that this summer was about to get a whole lot more complicated.

She hadn't planned on stopping at her dad's place. She had told herself that she'd just do a drive-by, maybe glance at the place from the road, and then check into the motel for the duration, or maybe see if one of the cabins was available at Pride's B&B. But as she passed the familiar turnoff, her hands tightened on the wheel, and before she could talk herself out of it, she was pulling into the gravel driveway, the sound of crunching rocks beneath her tires loud in the otherwise silent afternoon.

The home, a one-story log cabin, stood just as she had left it months before—quiet, untouched, and frozen in time. The once warm and inviting log walls now seemed darker, older. The wide front porch was coated in a thin layer of dirt and pine needles. The rocking chair by the door, where her father used to drink his morning coffee, sat motionless, tilted just slightly, as if waiting for him to return.

She shut off the engine and let out a shaky breath.

It felt wrong being here without him. Empty.

For the last year, this cabin had represented memories she had wanted to escape, a place filled with sadness she wasn't ready to face.

But there had been plenty of happy times before he had died. And now, something deep down caused her to reach for the car's door handle.

Even the air seemed, different. Stale.

When she stepped onto the porch, the wood creaked beneath her boots, the sound causing so many memories to replay in her head. She almost turned around and ran back to Portland.

Then she remembered why she was there, and she straightened her shoulders and stepped forward. The key was exactly where she remembered it, tucked beneath a loose plank of wood near the edge of the deck. She crouched down and brush away the dirt and debris before pulling it free. It was cold in her palm, the weight of it heavier than she'd expected.

Holding her breath, she unlocked the door, stepped inside, and flipped on the lights.

The air was thick with dust and the faint scent of pine and old wood. The living room was just as she had left it—an old couch against the far wall, a fireplace filled with cold ashes, and a wooden coffee table cluttered with magazines her dad had read through daily. A layer of dust coated every surface, proof that no one had stepped foot inside since the day she had locked the place up after his funeral.

She ran a hand along the back of the couch, her fingers leaving a clean streak in the dust. It was strange being here without him. Even after all the time away, the cabin still felt like his space, a place she had only borrowed.

Now it was hers.

The thought made her stomach twist.

She moved down the short hallway, pausing in front of the second door on the right. Her bedroom.

The door creaked as she pushed it open.

Nothing had changed.

There was the same twin bed with the faded blue comforter, the same wooden dresser with stickers she had slapped on as a teenager, the same books lined up neatly on the shelves above her desk. Most of them about true crime.

It was like stepping into the past, like the younger version of herself could walk through the door at any moment, still full of plans and dreams, still eager to leave Pride and never look back.

She sat down on the edge of the bed, her fingers curling into the old comforter.

Being here was even harder than she'd expected.

She had spent the last dozen months trying to move forward, trying to build a life separate from this place. Now she was back here for who knew how long. And worse, when the case was finally over and it came time to leave, she feared it wouldn't be easy, that she'd leave a piece of herself behind. Pride had a way of wrapping around you, changing you in quiet, permanent ways. Some of the people were just too easy to love, and they knew exactly how to pull you back.

She just knew that being here now, things would change. She could feel it in her bones.

When her stomach growled, she snapped back to reality. Staying here at the house was a heck of a lot cheaper than renting a cabin or staying in some hotel room, with who knows who for neighbors, so she brought in her two duffle bags and then headed into town to pick up some basic supplies.

First, to see if the rumors were true, she headed to Baked Pizzeria for food and gossip.

She had barely made it through the door when she heard that Abe Collins was indeed in town. Rumors had him staying the entire summer at his good friend Max Wilson's place. The writer and producer had purchased the lighthouse the previous year and had just finished remodeling the property ahead of his wedding to a local woman Dylan knew personally, Juliette Elliott. Juliette had been a few grades younger than her and, to her memory, had been kind.

Abe and Max had met a few years back on a movie shoot that Abe had played a small part in. Their friendship had bloomed fast.

Juliette's family ran the local coffee shop and bookstore, the Brew-Ha-Ha.

This was going to be easier than she'd expected. It was much simpler to spy in a small town where you knew everyone and there was lots of gossip to listen in on.

After grabbing a pizza to go, she hit the store for some basics and headed back to plan her next move.

She fell asleep on the sofa with her laptop in her lap after spending hours researching Abe's past. Or trying to, at any rate.

There was very little on his life before he had recorded his first album for Lucky Dog Studio, a huge label out of Texas, almost five years ago. From there, the man had become a household name. You couldn't listen to the radio without hearing one of his songs every half hour it seemed. His face was everywhere for the first couple years after his first record hit the charts. Billboards were filled with images of him modeling everything from underwear to cologne.

Then, about a year ago, everything changed. Rumors

started spreading about him buying a ranch in the country somewhere in California, and even though his music was still flooding the airways, his face was seen less.

She suspected the why of his disappearance, since a few articles had surfaced about his tragic past. Which, of course, was the reason she'd been hired.

The information on Abe's earlier life was fluff that he retold in every interview. Most of it was lies.

He *had* been raised by a single mother in a small town just outside of LA. He *was* an only child who had grown up on a horse ranch. He *was* a straight-A student who had taken a few college classes before dropping out to play music full time.

The lies were obvious to anyone who looked deeper.

He *hadn't* been discovered in a bar.

He had lucked out and been friends with two people who had made his career—Tony Carson, his PR manager, and James Lyle, producer to the rich and famous.

The three of them had met years before in college. Abe was best man at James's wedding six years back.

She figured the being-discovered story was good press.

After his underwear ads came out, several rumors circulated of romantic involvement.

Some claimed the relationship between Abe and Max was more than just a friendship. Others had him seeing a mysterious woman.

According to the minimal information she had found, Abe had met and started dating Kara Sinclair in college six years ago. Then, a year later, Kara had died in a car accident. That happened shortly after Abe finished recording his first album.

Kevin Sinclair, Kara's older brother, had hired Dylan to look into Abe's involvement in this accident. For the next few weeks while Abe was staying in Pride, her job was to get close to him and find the answers that Abe, no doubt, wanted to stay hidden.

Answers about the night he had possibly killed his girlfriend.

Chapter Two

"She's the one," Abe said, motioning to the young black and tan mare trotting circles in the small corral.

Max stood beside him with his arms crossed as he studied the horse with a skeptical look on his face. "You sure? She looks a little green."

Abe let out a low chuckle. "That's the point. She's young, but she's got good spunk. Good muscle tone." He narrowed his eyes and watched the horse trot around the coral. "She's a diva. Look at her demanding everyone's attention." He chuckled. "Give me a few weeks with her, and she'll be one of the best damn cutting horses in your barn."

Max exhaled through his nose, clearly still debating. Abe didn't blame him. Horses weren't cheap, and Max had already dropped a fortune on remodeling his new place. Including the massive barn that would house several horses, the first of which his friend planned on buying today. Thankfully, Abe knew what he was looking for. And this mare? She had the makings of a champion, even if she was up for auction for apparently being too wild.

The pair of them stood at the rail, watching as the auctioneer rattled off numbers in rapid succession. The mare tossed her head, ears twitching, as the crowd murmured around her. She was alert but not nervous, her hooves moving with a natural grace that made Abe nod again in approval.

"She's got good instincts," Abe added. "See the way she's watching everything? She's not just standing there, she's reading the pen. That's a horse that's got smarts."

Max sighed, running a hand through his hair. "Alright, alright. I'll bid." He lifted his auction paddle just as the price jumped.

Abe smirked. "Told you."

Max shot him a look. "If she throws me, I'm blaming you."

Abe chuckled again but didn't respond. When Max had the winning bid, his friend slapped him on the shoulder in celebration.

Then Abe focused on the next horse stepping into the ring, a tall, muscular buckskin gelding with a dark mane and intelligent eyes. The kind of horse that knew his own worth. He'd checked out both of the horses before the bidding started and had earmarked them for Max.

Actually, if he could, he'd purchase the gelding for himself. But he wasn't there to buy.

"Put a bid on him too," Abe said, nudging Max's arm.

Max groaned. "Another one?"

"You need a solid horse for yourself, don't you?" Abe shrugged. "That one's got strength. He'll be good for riding around that massive property you have. Plus, he won't spook easy."

Art of Love

Max hesitated, but when the bidding started, he raised his paddle again. The numbers climbed quickly, and Abe could see the internal struggle written all over Max's face.

Finally, with one last bid, the gavel slammed down. Sold.

Max exhaled. "Well, I guess I'm officially broke and own two horses."

Abe clapped a hand on his shoulder, grinning. "Nah, you just made two damn good investments."

Max shook his head, but there was amusement in his eyes. "If I go under, I'm making you dig me out."

"All you have to do is make another hit movie," Abe joked. Max laughed and slapped him on the shoulder.

They turned back to the corral as the next horse was led in, but Abe's attention drifted. Maybe it was just the auction buzz. Or maybe it was something else entirely.

He glanced around. The itch between his shoulder blades was back, the odd feeling of being watched. It was one of the reasons he'd needed the break and had promised to help Max out over the summer. One of the reasons at any rate. Avoiding questions was another.

He felt his jaw tense and had to force himself to relax as he and Max made their way up to the office to pay for the horses.

The auction office was small and smelled like old leather and coffee that had been sitting on the burner too long. Max handed over his check while Abe stood near the door, arms crossed, scanning the crowd outside through the glass window. The itch between his shoulder blades hadn't gone away.

"You alright?" Max asked as he signed the last of the paperwork.

Abe forced a smirk. "Yeah. Just not used to standing in one place for too long."

Max gave him a knowing look but didn't press. Instead, he tucked the receipt into his back pocket and pushed open the door. "C'mon, let's wait by the trailer. They should be bringing the horses out soon."

The sun was high, baking the dusty lot as they made their way to Max's truck and his new horse trailer, which were parked near the loading area. The low hum of conversations and the occasional call from the auctioneer still filled the air behind them, but out here, it was a lot quieter.

Abe leaned against the side of the truck, tugging the brim of his ball cap lower. Maybe he was being paranoid. He hadn't seen any cameras, no press lurking around, no obvious signs that anyone had followed him here. But he knew better than to let his guard down. Fame had a way of making a man feel like a fish in a damn glass bowl.

"Excuse me..."

Abe turned just as two young women, barely out of their teens, approached with shy smiles and wide, eager eyes. One clutched her phone, the other tugged at the hem of her tank top.

Oh, hell.

"You're Abe Collins, right?" the braver of the two asked, her cheeks already pink with excitement.

Max let out a quiet snort beside him, clearly enjoying this way too much. Abe shot him a glare before offering the girls a polite nod. "Yeah, that's me."

The girl with the phone practically bounced on her heels. "We thought it was you! My sister and I are huge fans. We saw you play in Portland last year. It was amazing."

Abe scratched at the back of his neck. "Appreciate that. Glad you enjoyed the show."

The second girl, the quieter one, spoke up. "Are you playing at the county fair this weekend?"

Abe shook his head. "Nah, not this year. Just here helping out a friend."

Both girls glanced over at Max, and Abe watched one of their jaws drop.

"You're Max Wilson!" Her smile grew. "Gosh, both of you here together. Could you both sign something for us?" The first girl lifted the hem of her white tank top, revealing a smooth stretch of skin above the waistband of her jeans. "We don't have anything else."

Max coughed, barely holding back a laugh.

"Yeah, alright." Abe shot him another glare.

He took their pen and signed their skin, careful to keep it above the fabric line so he wouldn't get accused of anything later. Max followed, choosing to sign his name on their sleeves instead.

"Thank you so much!" The girl beamed at him before turning to her sister. "Can we get a picture?" She waved her phone.

"Sure," he said and they both stood looking into her phone while she snapped a few photos of the four of them.

"I told you it was him!" He heard one say to the other as they giggled and hurried back off towards the auction barn.

Abe exhaled and rubbed a hand over his face. "Well, that was fun."

Max chuckled, opening the truck door to grab a water bottle. "Yeah. I found it highly entertaining. I always love being recognized."

Abe shot him a look as his friend dropped off.

"Right," he growled and lowered his hat some more in hopes that no one else would recognize him.

It wasn't like he wasn't used to this. He'd been dealing with fans for years now. But he had come here to lay low, not sign autographs in the middle of a damn horse auction.

Before Max could tease him further, a ranch hand leading two haltered horses emerged from the barn.

"There they are," Max said, stepping forward as the mare and gelding were brought over. The mare's ears twitched as she took in her new surroundings, while the buckskin gelding stood solid, steady as a rock. Yeah, he instantly knew he could fall for that horse.

Abe forced himself to shake off the lingering discomfort from the attention and focused on the horses instead.

At least with them, there were no expectations. No crowds. No cameras.

Just the familiar, steady rhythm of something real.

And right now, that was exactly what he needed. In the two days since he'd arrived in the small town, he'd gotten plenty of peace and quiet.

Shortly after unloading the horses in their new state-of-the-art stalls, complete with heated flooring and cameras, they headed down to the beach.

The timing for Max and Juliette's wedding had been perfect for him. He'd needed to get away from the city and all the new rumors. He'd arrived a few days early to help Max pick a few horses to fill his newly renovated barn.

Max had not only invited him to his wedding as best man but had suggested that he stay and watch over his property while Max and his new bride, Juliette, went on their honeymoon. He was pretty sure Max was taking pity on him after he found out some of the hell he'd been going through in the last few weeks.

They'd planned a small gathering that evening at a bonfire, or at least Max had said it would be small. Currently, there were more than a hundred townspeople gathered around two massive bonfires.

Abe stepped off the last stair and onto the beach and took in the sight before him. What was supposed to be a small get-together looked more like a full-blown festival. Two massive bonfires roared in the center of the beach between the water's edge and the tall grass. Flames licked at the night sky, shooting embers into the darkness. People milled about in clusters, some gathered near coolers packed with beer, others dancing to the twang of a guitar being played by someone near the fire. The low thump of music mixed with the sound of the waves crashing against the shore.

"Small gathering, huh?" Abe muttered, shooting a look at Max.

Max just grinned and clapped him on the back. "Welcome to Pride. When we celebrate, the whole town comes out."

Juliette appeared out of the crowd, barefoot, her white sundress flowing around her legs as she rushed into Max's arms. Abe stepped back, giving them a moment. They looked good together, he had to admit. Genuine. Happy.

Which meant he was officially the odd man out.

He'd liked Juliette from the moment he'd met her a few months back, when they had come to California for a movie premiere.

He grabbed a beer from a nearby cooler, took a long sip, and wandered towards one of the fires.

He was halfway through his drink when he noticed her.

She stood a little apart from the crowd, leaning against a driftwood log, arms crossed over her chest. She was wearing cut-off shorts and a faded band T-shirt and looked better than anything he'd seen in years.

The firelight cast a warm glow over her tanned skin, highlighting the sharp cut of her cheekbones and the loose waves of long hair that framed her face. There was something effortless about the way she held herself, like she belonged here but didn't feel the need to prove it.

Their eyes met, and for a brief second he expected recognition to flash on her face, like it usually did when people saw him. Maybe a flash of excitement. A whisper to a friend. The usual reaction when someone realized who he was.

But she just held his gaze, cool and uninterested, before looking away like he was just some guy at a party.

Well, damn. That was new.

Curious now, he watched her for a few more moments. She didn't appear to be with anyone. No one really stopped and talked to her or included her in their group conversations.

Almost five minutes later, he finally manned up and wandered over to her.

"You don't look like you're having much fun," he said, leaning on the log next to her.

She didn't glance over at him, instead she kept looking down into a drink. "Neither do you."

"Touché." His lips twitched.

There was a long pause before she finally looked at him, one of her dark brows lifting slightly. "So, are you a friend of the bride or groom?"

"Groom." He took another sip of his beer. "You?"

She shrugged. "Small towns. Everyone knows everyone."

"Right." He glanced around and then back when he noticed she was watching him.

"I'm Abe."

"Dylan."

She didn't offer a last name. Didn't gush about his music. Didn't even give him one of those lingering stares like most women did. Instead, she took a slow sip of whatever was in her cup and turned her attention back to the fire. Maybe she really didn't know who he was?

Lucky.

Abe studied her, intrigued despite himself. "So, you're from here?"

"Born and raised," she said a little dryly.

"You don't seem too interested in the town-wide party."

She let out a short laugh, finally turning her body towards him. "Let me guess. You think bonfire parties are all small towns do for fun?"

"Well... aren't they?"

That earned him a smirk. "We do other things too. We fish. Ride horses. Get in bar fights. Occasionally tip a cow or two."

"Seriously? That's a real thing?" Abe chuckled when she smirked. "Sounds like a wild time."

"We get by."

Silence stretched between them, but it wasn't uncomfortable. If anything, it was oddly easy. Abe couldn't remember the last time he'd had a conversation with someone who didn't expect anything from him. Who didn't try to impress him or make him feel like he owed them something just because of who he was.

Dylan took another sip of her drink, then gave him a once-over, finally showing the first sign of interest. "So, what's your story? Are you new in town, or just passing through?"

He could have given her the usual answer. The one he gave in interviews about how he was taking some time off, how he needed a break from the road, how he was looking for a little peace and quiet.

But for some reason, he just said, "A friend asked me to be his best man. He needed some help with horses, and then asked me to watch his place as he heads off on his honeymoon."

Dylan nodded like that made perfect sense. Then she smirked and motioned to the growing crowd. "Well, just a heads-up. If you're looking for peace and quiet, you came to the wrong place."

Abe laughed, tipping his beer in her direction. "Noted."

And for the first time in a long time, he didn't feel like the famous Abe Collins. Just a guy at a bonfire, flirting with a girl who didn't seem to care too much who he was.

And damn if that wasn't a nice change.

Then Max tapped on his shoulder and handed him a guitar. "Time to earn your room and board." He nodded as he realized everyone around them was watching and waiting on him. Well, damn. When he started singing, he glanced over at Dylan and was thankful she didn't seem all that surprised at how good he was.

Chapter Three

Just remain calm, Dylan kept telling herself as she rubbed knees with Abe while he sang one of her favorite songs of all time. Everyone in town was glued to his performance. Some even sang along when he got to the chorus.

With everyone in Pride in attendance, and with their eyes on the man sitting next her, she could no longer hide that she was back. She had heard about the bonfire earlier that morning at Sara's Nook and, since stepping onto the beach, she'd run into several people she knew.

She had managed to avoid long conversations the way she always did, by asking uncomfortable questions. After a few quick chats, she'd been left alone so she could get on with her job. Watching Abe.

The last thing she'd expected from the man was for him to actually cross the beach and start to flirt with her. Her. Boring Dylan. No-friends-on-the-planet Dylan.

She'd learned to hide her emotions over the years. Bullying, teasing, and name-calling no longer got under her skin. She had toughened up years ago and allowed nothing and no one to get through to her tender heart.

But damn if Abe Collins wasn't testing her resolve.

Dylan kept her face neutral, her body still, even as the heat from the fire and the man's presence beside her threatened to melt away the walls she'd spent years building. His voice—low, smooth, sexy as hell, and filled with something raw—wrapped around her, sinking into the parts of her she'd locked away long ago.

She wouldn't let him see it. Her nerves. Her doubts in herself. Wouldn't let him see that every note of the song sent a shiver down her spine. That the lyrics, which had once felt like they belonged to another world, now felt so personal.

He probably didn't even realize what he was doing to her.

The crowd around them had gone silent, completely mesmerized by the impromptu performance. People swayed, some singing along, some recording on their phones, but Dylan kept her focus on the fire, pretending like she wasn't sitting hip-to-hip with the man she'd spent years listening to in private.

Then, just as suddenly as it started, the song ended.

Cheers erupted. A few people whistled. Someone even called out, "Play another one!"

Abe chuckled, shaking his head as he handed the borrowed guitar back to its owner. "I think that's enough for tonight."

The crowed groaned but then turned back to chatting and dancing as someone else started playing the guitar.

Abe turned back towards her, eyes searching hers, like he was waiting for a reaction.

She refused to give him one.

"Not bad," she said, keeping her tone flat.

His lips twitched. "Not bad?"

She shrugged. "You've got a decent voice. A little rough around the edges."

That made him laugh. A real, genuine laugh that sent another ripple of awareness through her.

"Well, I'll take that as a compliment," he said, still grinning.

She didn't respond, just took a slow sip from her drink, pretending like his presence wasn't unraveling her carefully constructed indifference.

Then, just as she was about to push off the log and make her escape, someone in the crowd shouted, "Dylan! That *is* you. Are you back in town for good?"

A dozen heads turned towards her.

Damn.

She'd managed to avoid that question all night, and now, thanks to Abe freaking Collins sitting beside her, she had an audience.

Dylan forced a smile, keeping her voice light. "Just visiting."

The person, some guy she vaguely remembered from high school, nodded, but the way he was looking at her, and the way a few others whispered, told her the rumors would be swirling by morning.

She felt Abe watching her.

"So, you are not actually living here?" he asked, his voice quieter now.

"Didn't say that," she replied, standing and dusting the sand off her jeans.

He tilted his head, studying her like she was a puzzle he wanted to solve.

"Well," she said, nodding towards the bonfire, "enjoy the rest of the party, superstar."

Then she turned and walked away, refusing to look back.

Because if she did, she might just let him see the one thing she swore no one ever would. That he'd just shaken something loose inside her. And she had no idea how to put it back.

"That's it?" Abe fell in step with her.

She stopped and turned back towards him, her eyebrows arched. "What were you expecting? A standing ovation?"

He chuckled, shoving his hands into the pockets of his jeans. "Nah, just figured you'd at least pretend to be impressed."

"I don't pretend." She tilted her head, studying him. "So what's the deal? Do you always sing for free for your friends?"

He smirked. "Only when the mood strikes and he's letting me stay at his place."

She made a noncommittal sound and kept walking, the cool sand shifting beneath her bare feet. The party noise faded behind them as they moved closer to the water's edge, the waves rolling in with a steady rhythm.

"So, what's the deal with you?" he countered. "Do you always pretend not to care when a famous singer sits next to you?"

She didn't miss a step. Thankfully. "Depends on the singer."

His laugh was warm, easy. "Alright, I'll bite. Who impresses you?"

She gave him a slow, considering glance before shrugging. "People who are real. People who don't take themselves too seriously."

"Sounds like a low bar."

"You'd be surprised."

Abe watched her for a moment, as if trying to decide if she was messing with him or being completely serious. Then he nodded towards the water. "Why'd you leave Pride?"

Her jaw tightened for half a second before she smoothed it out. "Because I wanted to."

"That's not an answer."

"It's the only one you're getting."

Abe hummed in response, clearly not satisfied but letting it slide.

"Your turn," he said, kicking a small piece of driftwood. "Ask me something."

Dylan thought for a moment, then went for something easy. "What brought you here? Really."

He hesitated, just slightly, before answering, "I needed a break."

"From?"

He gave her a look. "That's two questions. My turn."

She rolled her eyes but let him have it.

"What do you do?" he asked.

Her heartbeat kicked up, but she kept her expression smooth as she embellished the truth. "Odd jobs. Whatever pays the bills."

His gaze sharpened. "That's vague."

"So was your answer."

He laughed again, shaking his head. "Alright, alright. Your turn."

She glanced at him out of the corner of her eye, watching the way the firelight in the distance cast shadows across his face. She knew she couldn't go in for the killer questions, so she tossed a light one to throw him off. "What's the best part of being famous?"

Abe thought about it, his expression shifting into something more thoughtful. "The music. Writing it. Playing it. The rest is just noise."

She was surprised but nodded, as if filing that answer away.

"My turn," he said, cutting his gaze towards her. "What's the worst part of coming back here?"

She stiffened, her feet pausing in the sand, and held in the answer that first came to mind. The people. Then, just as quickly, she smoothed it away. "Didn't say there was a worst part."

He didn't believe her. She could tell instantly. But he didn't push.

Instead, he let the moment settle between them, the sounds of the waves filling the silence.

Finally, she exhaled and took a step closer to the water. "Alright, one more question."

He arched a brow. "Make it a good one."

She turned to him, her dark eyes unreadable. "Why do you really have that look in your eyes? The look people have when they think no one is watching. The one that says you're running from something."

She knew that she had shaken him when he didn't answer right away.

"Like I said, I needed a break," he finally answered with a shrug. When she narrowed her eyes at him, he chuckled again. "How about I tell you the real reason I needed a break when you tell me the real reason you don't seem to enjoy being back home."

She nodded once and then took a deep breath as the water washed over her toes.

"How did you meet Max?" she asked, glancing over her shoulder as she heard the laughter behind them.

Abe's smile was quick and genuine. "We met on the set of *Never Enough*. I was brought in to help with the music score."

"The song you just played was the opening, right?" she asked.

He looked surprised and smiled. "You have heard of me then."

She dropped her guard and chuckled, "Who hasn't? I just didn't want to give you a big head."

He shifted and nudged her shoulder. "You're a hard nut to crack."

"Thanks," she said with a chuckle.

"Now that you know what I do for a living..."

She shook her head. "I've already told you."

His eyes narrowed. "Okay, then at least give me this one. What's the worst part about coming home?"

She sighed and glanced over her shoulder. "The people." His eyebrows arched in question. "Not that they're bad. It's just... they know me." She turned and wrapped her arms around herself. "Each and every person here knows everything there is to know about me. The good, the bad. Some of them have known me since birth." She sighed. "They saw me when I was..."—she glanced over at him—"not my best."

He nodded in understanding. "You're a private person. I get that. Believe it or not, I am as well."

She tilted her head and ran her eyes over him. "Must be hard when everyone in the world knows you."

"They think they know me," he corrected, his eyes moving to the dark waters.

Dylan watched him as he stared out at the water, his profile shadowed against the moonlight. There was something about the way he said it, the quiet weight behind his words, that made her chest tighten just a little.

She could relate.

People in this town thought they knew her, too.

She looked away, back towards the distant glow of the bonfire. Laughter echoed down the beach, voices blending together in a familiar hum. The past tugged at her like a rip current, trying to drag her under, but she planted her feet.

She wasn't that shy scared little girl anymore.

Was Abe a different person than the one who had been behind the wheel when Kara had died?

After all, this is what she was here for, right?

"So, do you ever get tired of it?" she asked finally, her voice softer than before.

His eyes flicked back to her. "Tired of what?"

"Being 'Abe Collins' all the time."

A slow, crooked smile tugged at the corner of his mouth, but it didn't quite reach his eyes. "More than you'd think."

Dylan let that settle between them, the rhythmic crash of the waves filling the silence.

After a moment, she nudged his arm with her elbow. "You know, for a big-time celebrity, you're not so bad."

His laughter was quiet but genuine. "And for someone who's been watching me, hiding that you know who I am, you're not very subtle."

Her breath caught, but she recovered quickly, rolling her eyes. "I have no idea what you're talking about."

"Uh-huh." He smirked and he shifted closer to her,

causing her stomach to dip at the way the word rolled off his tongue, but she forced herself to hold his gaze.

"I think you think too highly of yourself."

"Really?" He tilted his head, studying her. "Then why are you still here, Dylan?" He motioned to the party. "You could have left if you weren't having a good time."

For a moment, she considered telling him. Laying it all out, just to see his reaction.

But she didn't.

Instead, she gave him a smirk of her own. "That's another question. And I think we're out of time."

He let out an exaggerated sigh. "Shame. I was just starting to get somewhere with you."

She turned and started walking back towards the bonfire, tossing a look over her shoulder. "Maybe next time, rock star."

Abe grinned and followed her, something unreadable flickering in his gaze.

Dylan didn't look back again. Didn't trust that she wouldn't melt completely.

For the first time in a long time, she felt something stir in her chest. And she had no idea what to do about it.

Chapter Four

"Let go!" Max shouted at him. "She's not worth it." He stepped up on the rung of the corral.

"Like hell I will," he grunted, tightening his grip on the reins. "Come on, baby, we can do this." He squeezed his thighs a little harder.

The mare jerked under him and did a little sideways buck. But he held tight, his grip firm but steady as the mare fought against him. Her muscles coiled beneath him, her wild energy crackling like a live wire. He could feel her frustration, the way she tested his control, but he wasn't about to let go.

"Easy," he murmured, shifting his weight with her movements. "I know you've got more in you. Let it out now and be done with it."

The mare tossed her head, nostrils flaring, but he kept his hold on the reins, refusing to let her win.

"Abe!" Max's voice cut through the tension. "Damn it, man, don't be stupid. Just get down before she throws you."

Abe barely heard him. His focus was locked on the

horse beneath him, on the challenge of earning her trust, proving to her that he wasn't going anywhere.

She bucked again, harder this time, but he was ready. His body moved with hers, instinct kicking in. He'd been on enough stubborn horses in his lifetime to know that giving up wasn't an option.

"Come on, baby," he coaxed, loosening his grip just enough to give her the space to think, to choose. "You don't want to fight me. You just don't know me yet."

The mare's breathing came heavy, her sides heaving, but the wildness in her eyes flickered just for a second.

Abe exhaled slowly, keeping his voice calm. "That's it. You and me, we're gonna figure this out."

Another tense beat passed. Then, finally, she stilled beneath him, her muscles relaxing just a fraction.

Abe ran a hand down her neck, feeling the slight tremble there. "That's my girl."

Max let out a low whistle. "You're a damn lunatic, you know that?"

Abe grinned, reaching up to wipe the sweat from his forehead. "Takes one to know one."

Max shook his head, muttering something under his breath, but Abe could hear the relief in his voice.

He straightened in the saddle, giving the mare a final pat. "She just needed someone to believe in her."

Max snorted. "You always gotta make it poetic?"

Abe chuckled. "Only when it's true."

He took one last deep breath before easing the mare into a slow, careful walk around the corral. And as he did, he couldn't help but think that maybe he and this horse weren't so different.

He just needed someone to believe in him. Someone like Dylan.

Art of Love

He couldn't get the woman out of his mind, and that scared him. He was almost as spooked as the horse under him.

"You should have seen him," Max said between bites of pizza. "Just like the rodeo. I thought for sure he was going to fly through the air at any moment."

"I'm glad I didn't see it." Juliette laughed. "I probably would have screamed and spooked the horse even more."

"Naw, Stormy is chill," he said, causing them both to laugh.

"We haven't settled on her name yet," Max pointed out.

"Horses name themselves." He slapped Max on the shoulder.

"What's the other's one's name?" Juliette asked.

He thought about it then smiled. "Blaze."

"I like that," Juliette said. "Stormy and Blaze."

"Then it's settled." Max lifted his beer glass. "To Stormy and Blaze."

They all cheered and then drank.

"Oh!" Juliette cried out, then she jumped up and crossed the pizzeria.

They watched her go, and his heart did a skip in his chest when he saw her walk over and hug Dylan, who had just walked in.

For a split second, he saw Dylan drop her guard and smile and hug Juliette back. Then her eyes landed on him and the veil lifted again.

To his surprise, Juliette dragged Dylan over to their table.

"Max, Abe, this is Dylan Beck," Juliette said happily. "She's back in town for the summer. I missed talking to her the other night at the bonfire. Dylan, you have to sit with us after you get your food."

"Right," Dylan said, her eyes landing on him. "Sure."

He hid a smile by taking a sip of his beer.

Juliette sat back down next to Max, and the three of them chatted while they waited for Dylan to order.

"What does Dylan do for a living?" Max asked.

"I'm not sure. She was going to school for law, I think, the last time I heard. Her father died last year, leaving her this beautiful cabin and a ton of land up not far from our place," she told him.

He thought about the loss of his own dad. Not from death, but by absence. The man had never been part of his life.

"Does she have any other family? Siblings? What about her mother?" Max asked.

Juliette shook her head. "No, no one else. Her mother died in childbirth, along with her baby brother, a few years after she was born. Her father was the veterinarian in town way back when. He retired after being kicked in the chest by a cow. All I know is that the last few years of his life were pretty tough."

Abe leaned back in his chair, letting Juliette's words settle in. He glanced towards the counter where Dylan stood, her arms crossed as she waited for her order. She looked relaxed, but he'd spent enough time around guarded people to recognize when someone was holding back.

No family. No one left.

He understood that kind of loneliness. Maybe not in the same way, but enough to recognize it in someone else.

Max took a sip of his drink, his brow furrowed. "Tough how?"

Juliette sighed, lowering her voice. "I don't know the

full story, but I heard he struggled after his accident. He drank a lot. Isolated himself. Dylan was the one taking care of him towards the end, during those last few weeks." She shook her head. "She never really had it easy."

Abe's gaze drifted back to Dylan. There was something about her that intrigued him, something beyond her sharp wit and the way she acted like she didn't care who he was. She had an edge, a quiet strength, but there was also a weight there. A past she carried with her.

He knew what that was like.

The bell over the door chimed, and a couple of teenagers walked in, whispering and sneaking glances in his direction. Abe sighed. He'd been hoping to keep a low profile.

Dylan turned, her gaze flickering between him and the teens before she grabbed her pizza box and made her way back to the table.

"Looks like your fan club found you," she said, setting the box down and sliding into the booth next to him.

Abe smirked. "Looks like."

She arched an eyebrow. "You thought you could just waltz into town and no one would recognize you?"

He shrugged. "Worked for a couple days at least."

Dylan rolled her eyes, but there was a hint of amusement in them. She reached for a slice of pizza but paused when she noticed the look on Juliette's face.

"What?"

Juliette hesitated, then shook her head. "Nothing. Just... it's good to see you back."

Dylan didn't respond right away. Instead, she picked up her pizza and took a bite, chewing thoughtfully before finally saying, "Yeah. I'm not sure how long it will last."

Abe watched her carefully.

He wasn't sure why, but he suddenly found himself wanting to figure her out.

"But you are staying for our wedding, right?" Juliette took Max's hand. "I know we weren't very close, but I'd love it if you came."

"Yes, please," Max added. "Abe is going to do a full set at the after party."

"Sure, why not," Dylan said, stealing a glance in his direction. "I'm sure everyone is excited for another private concert."

Abe caught the flicker of something in Dylan's eyes. Was it sarcasm? Amusement? He couldn't quite tell, but it made him smile.

"Private concert might be a stretch," he said, leaning back in his seat. "I'm just playing a few songs. Just me and a guitar."

Max scoffed. "A few songs? Come on, man. You're doing a whole set. Including our first dance as husband and wife." He took Juliette's hand and lifted it to his lips and kissed her knuckles.

Abe shot him a look. "Save the mush for your wedding."

Max laughed. "Trust me, I have enough mush for before and after the wedding."

Abe didn't miss the way Dylan picked at the crust of her pizza, seemingly uninterested. Unlike everyone else in town, she wasn't fawning over the idea of him playing. Hell, she hadn't even reacted when Max first mentioned it. That only made him more curious about her.

"So, at least you're sticking around town for a short while," he said, watching her closely.

Dylan shrugged. "Yeah, I guess for now."

Vague. Noncommittal. He recognized the move—keep people at arm's length so they don't get too comfortable. It was something he'd done himself more times than he could count.

Juliette beamed. "That's great! Maybe we can catch up before the wedding. You still like hiking?"

A brief hesitation. Then, "Yeah. Sometimes."

Abe didn't miss the way Dylan shifted in her seat, like she was ready for the conversation to be over. She wasn't one for small talk, that much was obvious.

The bell above the door chimed again, and this time, it wasn't just a couple of teenagers sneaking glances at him. It was a large group of people whispering and pointing in his direction.

Dylan noticed too. She arched an eyebrow and leaned in slightly, her voice low enough for only him to hear. "You always have this much trouble enjoying a slice of pizza?"

He let out a short laugh. "Depends on where I am."

"Guess you should've worn a hat."

He smirked. "Guess so."

Juliette and Max were already chatting with some of the newcomers, who were clearly working up the courage to ask him for an autograph.

Dylan stood. "Well, this has been fun, but I should get going."

Abe felt an unexpected pang of disappointment. He wasn't ready for her to leave just yet.

"Where's the fire?" he asked.

She tilted her head at him and grabbed her pizza. "See you around, superstar."

And with that, she walked out. He watched her go as he started signing autographs for the group of teens.

Chapter Five

What the hell was she doing here? She smoothed down the silk dress she'd hastily purchased in Edgeview yesterday. She'd planned on skipping the main event, but something told her that it might be a good time for Abe to let his guard down.

So she'd purchased a modest dress and slapped on the most uncomfortable shoes she owned. The moment she parked her car at Sunset Event's large barn, she second-guessed her outfit choice. Especially when a couple of women walked past her wearing very skimpy dresses that showed a hell of a lot more skin than hers did.

Dylan let out a slow breath, adjusted the strap of her dress, and stepped out of the car. The moment the cool night air touched her skin, she considered turning right back around.

This was a mistake.

She wasn't one for fancy events, and she sure as hell wasn't one for parties where everyone knew everyone. It was bad enough she'd spent most of the bonfire dodging small talk and pretending she didn't recognize half the town and Abe. Now she was walking straight into the lion's den, dressed in silk and strapped into heels that felt more like medieval torture devices than footwear.

But she wasn't here for fun or comfort.

She was here to work.

Abe Collins was her job, and if she wanted to get a read on him and find out what Kevin Sinclair had hired her to find out, then she needed to see him in his element. Relaxed. Unfiltered.

Still, as she moved towards the barn doors, she couldn't shake the feeling that she was out of place. Women strutted past her in barely-there dresses, all legs and confidence. She felt like a fraud playing dress-up.

Get it together, Dylan, she berated herself.

During her years as a PI, she'd played many roles. This was just another one. With a quick inhale, she straightened her shoulders and walked inside.

The massive barn had been transformed years ago into one of the best event venues along the coast. Strings of twinkling lights hung from posts outside the doors, casting a warm, golden glow over the entire entryway.

The wedding portion of the night was to be held just outside the barn, on the beach. There were signs and tiki torches that led guests down the pathway to the sand.

Many guests were already seated in the rows of chairs, so she slipped in and sat at the back on the bride's side.

Soft music floated through the air, blending with the rhythmic crash of waves against the shore. The sun hung low in the sky, painting the horizon in warm hues of orange and pink. A gentle breeze carried the scent of salt and flowers, and ruffled the white linen draped over the wedding arch at the front of the aisle.

Art of Love

Dylan took in the picturesque scene. The chairs were arranged in neat rows, filled with many familiar faces from town.

She'd never been one to dream about the perfect wedding, but this was a damned good spot for it.

Nothing seemed out of place.

The music changed, and Max appeared near the front, along with a priest. He stood there near the arch, grinning like it was his best day. His usual easygoing demeanor had been replaced with something deeper, an emotion that softened his features as he watched the pathway leading to the aisle.

Abe suddenly appeared, a pretty brunette on his arm. The woman looked familiar.

Dylan narrowed her eyes and tried hard to place her. But her eyes kept returning to Abe.

Damn. The man looked sexy as hell in a monkey suit. She enjoyed the view as other bridesmaids and groomsmen walked down the aisle. When the music changed again, everyone stood up.

All eyes turned towards the barn as the large wooden doors swung open.

Juliette appeared, radiant in a flowing lace gown, her hair in long curls pinned back with delicate pearls. Her father, Rafe Elliott, walked beside her, his expression a mix of pride and nostalgia as he led her towards the man waiting for her.

Dylan's heart sank when she suddenly realized that her own father wouldn't be around for her special moment. Not that she'd ever have a day like this. Hell, she'd never even gone out on a second date with a man before, let alone seen someone long enough to think about spending the rest of her life with them.

She had faced the facts years ago—she wasn't the marrying type.

Max's breath visibly hitched as Juliette stepped onto the pathway. His fingers curled at his sides, and for a moment, he looked as though he might take a step forward, as if he couldn't bear to wait another second to be with the woman he loved.

Dylan felt something stir inside her. Weddings weren't usually her thing. Too many emotions, too much attention on one moment. But there was something about this one. The way Max looked at Juliette, like she was his entire world. Like nothing else existed beyond her.

Juliette's father placed a gentle kiss on her cheek before stepping back, and Max stepped forward and immediately took her hands.

As the officiant began to speak, her gaze flickered to Abe, who stood watching the couple exchange vows with an unreadable expression on his face.

She wondered what he was thinking, if he'd ever looked at someone the way Max looked at Juliette. Had he looked at Kara like that? Had her death caused his world to sink and disappear?

She dove deep into those thoughts as the vows were exchanged, as a mixture of laughter and teary-eyed promises were shared. When the officiant finally pronounced them husband and wife, cheers erupted as Max pulled Juliette into a romantic kiss, lifting her slightly off the ground as the waves crashed behind them.

Dylan found herself clapping along with the crowd, despite her dark, selfish thoughts.

Maybe she didn't believe in fairytales, but even she had to admit this one felt pretty damn good.

Art of Love

Guests waited as the couple made it down the aisle, followed by the best man, groomsmen, and bridesmaids.

She hid out of sight as Abe walked by, and then she suddenly realized it was Sophia, Juliette's best friend, whom he had been walking with. The girl had moved to Pride shortly after her sixteenth birthday. Her brother, Lucas, owned the Mexican restaurant in town.

Out of the near one hundred kids that had been in her class during school, these two girls had been most like her, an outsider. Most important, they'd been kind to her. It was one of the reasons she'd agreed to come to the wedding in the first place.

She followed all the other guests back down the sandy pathway and into the barn.

There, a live band started to play on the stage in the corner, though they were nowhere near as good as the actual superstar that was somewhere in the crowd. The air buzzed with laughter and clinking glasses as champagne was passed out, and for a moment, Dylan let herself take it all in.

She spotted Max and Juliette and the wedding party and family members upstairs, posing for photos.

Deciding she needed a beer, she headed to the bar. She leaned on the counter as she waited to place her order.

"Hey," someone said behind her. She glanced over and held in a groan.

Tommy Leif had been an all-star-player in every sport. He was a jock through and through. And one of Dylan's worst nightmares. The amount of teasing she had received from this boy alone left deep scars that still stung today.

"Hey, Tommy."

"Tom," he corrected, his eyes narrowing. "Holy shit, it *is* you. Dylan Beck." He said her name like an announcer at a prize fight and shook his head, as if not believing his eyes.

"In the flesh," she replied dryly as she waved at the bartender, praying the woman would come over and take her order soon. If Tommy was going to be the first one she talked to tonight, she knew it was going to be a very long night. Maybe she needed something stronger than a beer.

"Yeah, and such pretty flesh it has become," Tommy purred as he leaned on the counter and ran a fingertip down her arm. She cringed.

"You don't want to touch me, Tommy," she said clearly.

His eyebrows shot up.

It wasn't that Tommy, or Tom, wasn't good-looking. He fit the image of the all-American small-town hero to the tee. Blond hair, sexy blue eyes that some women instantly fell for, dimples when he smiled, and a body that everyone in town knew well, thanks to his many shirtless runs through town.

"I heard you were back in town for a while." He leaned closer. "Care to have some fun while you're here?"

"No thanks," she said, waving again at the bartender.

"No?" Tommy lowered his voice. "I always thought you were stuck-up. How about you prove me wrong?"

"No, thanks," she said again, this time getting the bartender's attention.

"Whiskey, straight, and a beer. Any beer," she added.

When Tommy's fingers wrapped around her upper arm, she stilled. "Come on, Dylan, we all know how much you wanted to get with me back in the day."

She turned slightly until she was nose to nose with Tommy. "Like I said, you don't want to touch me." She glanced down at his fingers and winced when they tightened.

"Oh yeah." Tommy smiled, showing off those dimples. "I like challenges." He moved closer until his body was practically plastered against hers.

Even though the bar area was packed, she knew there was enough room for her to take a step back. Instead, she shifted slightly until her knee came up tight against his groin.

"Oh yeah, I knew you'd be fun." He chuckled.

Then she shifted and he winced. "Tommy, you've got about three seconds to let go of me before you find out what I spent five years learning in self-defense classes." She smiled brightly.

His eyebrows lowered. "Like I said..."

"One," she started, and his smile grew.

"I like..."

"Two." She tilted her head and moved her knee slightly to the right, causing him to wince again.

His hand dropped to his side.

"Maybe some other time." He abruptly turned and walked away.

"Here you are." The bartender set down her shot and a beer.

Dylan downed the whiskey, enjoying the burn for a moment before taking a sip of the cold beer.

She glanced around, wondering how many more times Tommy would hit on her that evening. The guy had never been one to take no for an answer. Something told her he hadn't changed all that much.

Standing by the bar, she scanned the crowd as people settled at tables or stood around sipping drinks while they waited for the wedding party to finish taking photos.

No sign of Abe yet.

After a few moments, she took her beer and skirted the

edge of the room, avoiding the dance floor entirely, and made her way towards a quieter corner near the outdoor patio. From here, she could watch the crowd of people come and go without being seen.

She was scanning the faces when a familiar voice rumbled behind her.

"Do you want me to break the guy's nose?"

Dylan turned slightly to her right, meeting Abe's inquisitive gaze.

Just the sight of him had her heart jumping in her chest. Damn, she had better get that under control.

He looked... different. Not just because he'd ditched the jacket and tie and had unbuttoned a few buttons on his shirt. There was something unreadable in his eyes.

She smirked, tilting her head, and tried to play it cool. "Which guy?"

His lips quirked. "The one who wouldn't take his hands off you at the bar."

So he'd been watching her and had witnessed the scene with Tommy?

Dylan let her eyes drift over him, lingering just long enough to make it clear that she'd noticed his attention. "No. I can handle myself."

"Is he an old boyfriend?"

She couldn't help the burst of laughter that escaped her lips. "He wishes." She took a sip of her beer.

"Did you come here alone?" he asked, glancing around.

She nodded slowly. "What about you? Is there someone waiting in the wings?" She made a show of looking around too.

He smiled. "Nope, all alone."

"I bet if you wait a few minutes, there'll be plenty of women lined up to fill your dance card."

He chuckled and then glanced around, his expression unreadable until it landed on her again. "I think I already spotted something I like."

"It must be exhausting," she mused, sipping her beer again.

He arched a brow. "What?"

"Playing the part of the smooth superstar."

He laughed and then studied her, and for a second, she thought he might deflect. Instead, he let out a slow breath and leaned against the wall beside her. "Yeah. Sometimes."

Dylan nodded, watching him carefully. Was he really letting his guard down?

Now might be her chance.

But just as she opened her mouth, everyone in the room started to cheer as the bride and groom slowly made their way down the stairs.

For the next half hour, Abe was busy fulfilling his best-man duties. He toasted the happy couple, stood by as they thanked everyone and the father of the bride said words, and then sat at the main table as everyone was served dinner.

When the happy couple cut into the cake, he disappeared.

Shortly after, Abe stepped up to the microphone on stage, he glanced over the crowd before turning his attention to Max and Juliette, who stood near the dance floor, hands intertwined. The warm glow of string lights cast a golden hue over them, making the moment feel even more surreal.

He tapped the mic lightly. "Alright, everyone, it's time for the moment we've all been waiting for, the first dance." A few cheers and whistles rang out. "Now, I've only known Max for a few years, but I've never seen him as happy as he is with Juliette. She's made him a better man, and frankly, I think we all owe her a thank-you for that." Laughter rippled through the crowd as Max shook his head with a smirk.

Abe's grin softened as he looked at Juliette. "And Juliette, you're one of the most amazing people I've had the pleasure of knowing. You two found something rare, something real. So tonight, let's celebrate that." He nodded towards the dance floor. "Now, if the bride and groom would take their places, I've got a little something special for them."

The guests clapped as Max led Juliette onto the dance floor. The band played a soft instrumental intro as Abe adjusted his guitar strap and stepped closer to the mic and started to play. Taking a steadying breath, he began to sing.

The song was new. Or at least she hadn't heard it before. It wasn't about fame or heartbreak or the kind of love that came and went with the seasons. It was about something deeper. Something lasting.

His voice carried over the crowd, rich and steady, each lyric laced with emotion:

It's not in the words we say, but the way we hold on tight...

Through the storms, through the quiet, through the long and endless nights...

When the world fades away, when it's just you and me...

That's where love is, that's where we're meant to be...

Dylan watched as Max and Juliette swayed together, lost in each other. The way Max's hand held Juliette close, the way her head rested against his shoulder—it was the kind of moment people spent lifetimes chasing.

It caused Dylan's heart to ache. Suddenly, she realized just how much she'd lost or given up over the years. None of it had mattered to her before now.

Coming back to Pride had been a huge mistake. Taking

this job had been an even bigger one. She'd been doomed since the moment she'd found out who she was supposed to be looking into. After all, she'd lost her heart to the man the first moment she'd heard him sing years ago.

What in the hell was she supposed to do now?

Chapter Six

As his last song in the hour-long set came to an end, the guests erupted into applause, but he barely heard it. His gaze drifted over the crowd, searching for the one person he wanted to see. His chest tightened slightly when he spotted Dylan sitting quietly near the edge of the large room.

She wasn't clapping.

She was just watching him.

And for the first time in a long while, he felt like someone was seeing more than just the famous man on stage.

When their eyes locked, he stilled, realizing the sad look in her eyes wasn't because of his lyrics.

He saw her blink once, twice, then she jumped up and made a beeline towards the doors.

"That's it for me tonight, but don't worry," he said as the crowd booed, "the band still has plenty of songs left in them and will get things moving and shaking." He set down the guitar. "Kick it up a notch," he told the guys, and quickly exited the stage.

To avoid the many well-wishers and fans, he side-stepped through the kitchen and exited through the back door, circling around the building in search of Dylan.

He found her sitting on a swing near what appeared to be the smoking area.

"Need a light?" he asked, sitting next to her.

"I don't smoke. You?" She glanced at him and then set the swing moving.

"Nope." He sighed and glanced up at the stars. "Nice night." She remained quiet. "Was I that bad?" he asked, sparing a glance at her.

She stopped the swing and turned towards him, a questioning look on her face.

"You left pretty fast," he pointed out.

"The room was stuffy." She crossed her arms over her chest.

"Right." He set the swing moving again. "It's funny, after my third album, I stopped worrying if people would enjoy my new songs."

Dylan tilted her head slightly, studying him in that way that made him feel like she was peeling back layers he hadn't even realized he had. "Why?"

He exhaled, watching a cloud shift in front of the moon, dimming its light for a moment. "Because at some point, you stop chasing approval. You realize you'll never please everyone, so you stop trying." He shrugged. "I wrote that new song for them." He nodded towards the reception, where the sound of laughter and music still drifted through the night. "But if they'd hated it, I wouldn't have changed a damn thing."

She held his gaze for a long moment before shifting her focus back to the sky. "That's an interesting way of looking at things."

Abe shrugged. "You don't agree?"

She gave him a half shrug. "I think people tell themselves they don't care what others think, but deep down, everyone does. At least a little."

"Even you?" he challenged.

Her lips quirked, and she shrugged slightly, but she didn't answer.

A comfortable silence stretched between them, broken only by the distant hum of the wedding festivities. The night air was cool, carrying the salty scent of the ocean.

He glanced at her, the way the wind teased a loose strand of hair across her face, the way she sat calm, collected, unreadable. She intrigued him in a way he hadn't expected.

"I may not really care what others think about my set, but I really want to know what you think," he admitted

She hesitated, as if weighing her words. "Everyone seemed to enjoy it."

He grinned. "That's not an answer."

She sighed. "Fine. It was good." She gave him a side-eye. "Very good."

He leaned back, setting the swing in motion again. "I'll take that compliment."

She shook her head, amusement flickering in her eyes before she glanced away.

For the first time in a long while, Abe wasn't worried about the crowd waiting for him inside or the guests who'd want autographs or pictures with him. Right now, all he cared about was sitting here, in the quiet, with the one person who didn't seem to give a damn who he was.

For some reason, that felt more important than anything else.

He let the silence hang for a moment, the steady sway

of the swing matching the rhythm of the waves in the distance. He turned towards her slightly, catching the curve of her profile in the moonlight.

"You always this hard to impress?" he asked, his voice low and teasing.

She smirked, not looking at him. "Only when someone's trying really hard to impress me."

"Damn," he said with a soft laugh. "I thought I was being subtle."

"Oh, you're about as subtle as a bull in a china shop."

He leaned in a little, his shoulder brushing hers. "Good thing I like a challenge."

That earned him a glance that was sharp but not unkind. "That's the second time I've heard that tonight." She shook her head quickly. "Do you flirt with everyone who doesn't fawn over you?"

He hated knowing that he had used the same line as the blond man who had been obviously flirting with Dylan at the bar.

"Nope," he said, eyes locked on hers now. "Just the ones I want to get to know."

She opened her mouth to say something, but before she could speak, a couple of people turned on the pathway and headed towards them.

"There you are!" a loud voice called, followed by the shuffle of heels on gravel. "Abe! We were wondering where you snuck off to."

He tensed slightly as two very drunk women in cocktail dresses approached, smiling too widely at him. One clutched her phone like it was a backstage pass.

Dylan shifted beside him, and he felt the magic moment fracture.

"Sorry to interrupt," the taller one said, her gaze darting from him to Dylan and back. "But could we get a quick photo? My mom is going to freak when she sees it."

Abe stood slowly, offering a polite smile even as he glanced down at Dylan. "Give me one sec?"

She nodded slightly, that unreadable mask slipping back into place.

He stepped away, posed, signed something on one of their phone cases, and made all the right small talk, but his eyes kept drifting back to the swing.

By the time he turned around, she was already walking away, her bare shoulders catching the moonlight as she disappeared around the corner of the barn.

"Shit," he muttered under his breath.

The night had been perfect, until it wasn't. And he had the sinking feeling he'd just let something real slip through his fingers.

When he went back inside, it was to even more photo and signature requests. He tried to convince everyone that the night was for Max and Juliette, but they kept surrounding him.

Finally, he broke free and, to avoid the swarm of fans, he headed up to the balcony and watched the scene from above. He enjoyed watching his friend, who was more than a little drunk and really enjoyed dancing slowly with his new wife.

He didn't see Dylan again and wondered if she'd left after they'd chatted. He'd agreed to help clean up after Max and Juliette drove away in the limo to head out on their two week honeymoon, so he spent until just after one in the morning loading all their presents and other items into his truck to take back to the house.

Babysitting their place while they were gone wasn't going to be much of a hardship. He needed the seclusion and the quiet and really enjoyed the newly remodeled home.

The attached lighthouse was a great bonus.

His mind kept returning to the conversations he'd had with Dylan. The way her eyes watched him as he spoke. Not with awe, like all the other women, but with interest. It was almost as if she was assessing everything he said, like it was important. He'd never had that before.

He pulled into Max and Juliette's gravel driveway just after one-thirty in the morning, the headlights casting long, dancing shadows over the front of the buildings. The horses were no doubt asleep in the quiet barn, and the night air was still, heavy with salt and summer.

A full moon hung in the cloudless sky. He parked near the front steps, climbed out, and took a deep breath. He stared up at the star-filled sky for a moment before he started unloading the mountain of wedding gifts.

He moved on autopilot as he stacked boxes inside the front hallway. His muscles were tired and his feet ached, but his mind was elsewhere. On Dylan. On the way she didn't try to flatter him or appease him. Her words carried weight. He liked that.

He was setting down the last wrapped box when something inside the house shifted.

A soft creak.

A muffled footstep.

Abe froze.

He glanced towards the stairs, his heart suddenly thudding against his ribs. The light flickered above him as he stepped towards the sound.

He hadn't been quiet before, so if someone was in there, they knew he was there.

Inside, the old house was quiet, save for the soft ticking of the antique clock in the entryway.

A second noise, upstairs this time. Light. Quick. Like someone trying not to be heard.

He didn't call out. He just moved silently, grabbing a fireplace poker from beside the stone hearth as he crept down the hallway towards the stairs. At the top, the hallway stretched in both directions, moonlight streaming in from a window at the end.

For a split second, he thought he saw an old man standing under the light. Then he blinked and realized it was a painting that hung on the wall. His heart started beating again, but then there was another soft noise. Another shuffle.

He moved towards Max's office just as a shadow darted from the spare bedroom he'd been staying in. He froze for a split second, then followed suit as the figure raced out of the open doorway in Max and Juliette's bedroom.

"Hey!" he shouted, and rushed after the shadow, arriving on the deck just in time to see the figure in dark clothing sprinting across the backyard, heading for the tree line.

He cursed, leaning over the railing to try to get a better look, but the figure had disappeared into the night, swallowed by the trees and brush.

He rushed back through the house, flipping on every light and sweeping each room methodically. Nothing was missing. Nothing was out of place. Whoever it was, they hadn't taken anything. Or maybe they hadn't found what they were looking for.

Abe stood in the middle of the room he'd been staying in, jaw clenched. His grip on the fireplace poker had tightened without him realizing it. The adrenaline was fading, and a chill crept down his spine.

Was it just a coincidence that they had been in his room? One of the drawers to the nightstand was opened slightly. Leaning down, he opened it and instantly knew that it was the noise he'd heard, alerting him earlier.

Nothing was in there except a book he'd borrowed from Max's library and had started reading two nights before. He looked in the other nightstand, where he kept his phone charger, his wallet when he was there, and some condoms, just in case.

Sitting on the edge of the bed, he felt another shiver race down his back. In the end, he decided not to tell Max and Juliette. Not yet. They deserved peace on their honeymoon, not a panic. Instead, he made a mental note to check the new security system Max had installed, and shown him how to use, first thing in the morning.

Just to be safe. But right now, he was exhausted.

Over the next half hour, he made sure the horses were okay and double-checked every window and door before crawling into bed around three in the morning.

The next day, after feeding the horses and gulping down two cups of bitter black coffee, Abe sat at Max's desk and pulled up the camera feeds on the large monitor.

The timestamp blinked.

12:47 a.m.–2:13 a.m.

The footage was missing. Not blacked out. Not fuzzy. Just missing.

He stared at the screen for a long time.

All of the footage was just... gone. No recordings. Just a dead space.

Whoever had been inside the house knew what they were doing.

And that unsettled him more than anything else.

Was this about all the recent questions from the press about his past? He shivered. Did this have anything to do with Kara?

Chapter Seven

That was stupid! Dylan told herself as she stopped just beyond the tree line to take a couple of deep breaths. Her heart pounded against her ribs like a warning drum, and her legs ached from sprinting across the field. She knew she'd taken too long searching his room.

Way too long.

The moment she'd heard the truck pull up the gravel drive, she'd frozen, hands deep in the drawer of a nightstand in Max's guest room, the one Abe had been staying in. Of course it had taken her a while to find out which of the rooms he had moved into at first. More time wasted.

Then, he had returned and she hadn't even had time to fully process the sound before instinct kicked in, telling her to run.

And she had.

She'd bolted through the glass doors she'd easily opened earlier and rushed down the back slope like some sort of criminal.

Because she was one. When the occasion called for it.

Trespassing. Breaking and entering. Snooping through someone's private things in hopes of finding answers to a case no one even wanted reopened. She'd even made sure to use the jammer for the security system she'd spied when she'd cased the place a few nights ago.

Now, back in her car, which she'd parked at the public beach access a mile away, she peeled off her gloves and stocking hat and tossed them onto the passenger seat as she gripped the steering wheel tight. The world around her remained dark and still. Such was life in a small town.

She shifted into gear and slowly drove away, keeping her headlights off until she was well out of sight from the house.

The back roads twisted through the hills as she made her way towards her father's cabin. Her cabin now. Her thoughts spun faster than the tires on the wet pavement.

Had he seen her?

She didn't think so. She'd been careful. But the way the porch light had shone on her had her second-guessing everything.

You were too curious, she scolded herself. You asked him about the journal. You should've waited to see what he shared willingly. Now he'll know something's off.

But what was she supposed to do? Sit around and wait for him to hand her a clue?

Earlier that night, she'd slipped the question in casually enough. "Do you write your lyrics down? Or do you just remember them?" and watched his face carefully.

"I have a journal I keep lyrics in," he had answered.

"Do you take it everywhere you go?"

He'd opened his mouth to answer. She could see it, the shift in his eyes. Something about that question had struck a nerve.

But before he could respond, a wedding guest interrupted them, and the moment had vanished.

And now? She had nothing to show for her search. No journal. No ties to Kara Sinclair.

Just a room far neater than any musician's space had a right to be. Organized. Bare. Like he'd purposefully left out anything worth finding. Maybe she should take a trip to his ranch in California?

No. His security was far too tight there. She'd read an article where a few fans had tried to break in and hadn't even made it past the gate before his full-time security team had stopped them.

She turned off onto the long gravel drive leading to her cabin and parked in the shadowed curve of the garage. She sat in the stillness for a long minute, fingers resting on the keys, her thoughts looping back to the single photograph she had found tucked in the pages of a novel on the nightstand.

It had been old. Faded.

Abe, a few years younger. Smiling. Standing beside Kara.

They looked so in love with one another it hurt.

If he was what everyone thought he was, then why in the hell would he still have that?

He claimed in one of his first interviews not to have known Kara well. He claimed it was just a college fling.

But that photo told a different story. Most men don't keep a photo from a fling.

The song he had sung for Max and Juliette also told a different story. At first, anyone would believe the lyrics were for the happy couple. But she somehow knew they weren't. He never mentioned her name, but Kara was the real inspiration for the romantic song.

Dylan bit her lip, her hand trembling slightly as she finally shut off the engine.

She had to be careful now. Smarter. She couldn't afford any more mistakes.

Because something told her that Abe might be more involved in Kara's death than he let on. And it made her sick to her stomach.

The next morning, she took a jog on the beach. She had her headphones in, listening to her favorite tunes as she sprinted up and down the stretch of sand.

Her mind kept circling back to the night before—the swing, the starlight, the way Abe had looked at her like she was the only person in the world who mattered. It annoyed her. Not just because she hadn't found anything in his room, or because he'd nearly caught her sneaking away like a thief in the night, but because she felt something.

And one thing life had taught her was that feelings were dangerous.

She jogged until her legs burned and her lungs stung, only stopping once the sun rose high enough to kiss her skin with warmth. After a few stretches and a cool drink of water from the bottle she'd stashed in her trunk, she slipped a lightweight hoodie over her tank top and headed into town, hoping for a little caffeine and something sweet to go with the growing ache in her chest.

Sara's Nook was already buzzing when she stepped inside. The smell of coffee and freshly baked scones hit her like a hug from an old friend. She made her way to the counter and was halfway through ordering her usual—black coffee and a lemon blueberry scone—when a familiar voice cut through the hum of conversation.

"Well, well. If it isn't the fastest girl on the beach."

Dylan turned and found herself staring up at Nate Elliott. He looked exactly the same as he had in high school, only broader in the shoulders and maybe a little more confident in his smile. His dark sandy hair was wind-tousled, and his gray T-shirt clung to a chest that definitely saw time in a gym.

She had seen him at the wedding but hadn't talked to him. Not because he was one of the bad ones in town. He had just been too busy with his sister Juliette's wedding.

"Nate," she said, offering a polite smile. "You're up early. After last night's party, I would have thought you'd be MIA like most of the town is."

He chuckled. "Naw, old habits from my track days have me up running almost every day." He shrugged.

"I heard that you lived in the city?"

He grinned and held up a coffee cup. "I moved back a few weeks ago. I saw you running and tried catching you out on the sand, but you're still as fast as you were in track."

"And you're still too slow," she joked.

He nodded slightly. "Caffeine is survival."

She chuckled and took a step to the side so he could place his order. "You just moved back from…"

"Portland. I moved back to help out with the family business. You know how it goes. Once you're in, you're in for life."

"Yeah," she murmured, eyes flicking out of the windows to the Brew-Ha-Ha book store, which sat down and across the street a little. "Small towns have a way of pulling you back."

He leaned against the counter, giving her a once-over that was probably meant to be subtle but wasn't. "So, you here to stay, or just visiting?"

"I'm... figuring that out." She had decided to keep things vague with anyone who asked her.

He smiled, easy and warm. "Well, if you're around for a while, maybe we could grab dinner. Catch up properly."

It was a tempting offer. Nate had always been kind to her in school, never mocking her the way others had. And now he was single, good-looking, and clearly interested.

But even as she considered saying yes, her mind betrayed her. She pictured Abe's eyes on hers, the way his voice had softened when he said her name, how close they'd come to something that almost felt like... more.

"I'll think about it," she said, taking her coffee from the barista with a grateful nod.

"Good," Nate said, flashing her another charming grin. "I'll hold you to that." He took up his coffee cup, and as he turned to leave she found herself watching him walk away. Objectively, he checked all the boxes. And yet... the flutter in her chest that came when Abe so much as looked at her wasn't there.

And that was more confusing than anything else.

She took a bite of her scone after settling at a corner table by the window. She pulled out her phone and opened the photo she'd taken of the one thing she had found the night before: the old picture of Abe and Kara.

Answers were out there.

She just had to stop letting certain feelings get in the way of finding them.

After finishing her coffee and scone at the bakery, she tucked the pastry bag that held two more scones under her arm and crossed the street to the grocery store. The place had changed a lot since she'd left town, and she was surprised to find herself smiling at the improvements. The windows were new, the signage bigger, and the smell of fresh bread drifted out the automatic doors as she stepped inside.

Since Wyatt Auston had taken over after Patty O'Neil passed, the store had been transformed. What had once been a cramped and dusty little shop was now buzzing with energy. There were digital checkout lanes, a newly remodeled deli section, and even catering and delivery services, things Dylan never would have imagined seeing in the small town.

These days, with her energy low and her focus elsewhere, she found herself relying more and more on the ready-made meals from the deli. She made a beeline for the prepped salads and hot food and grabbed a few things for tomorrow's breakfast.

She was halfway through scanning the fresh pasta selection when a child's giggle caught her attention.

"Dylan! Stop pulling on Mommy's necklace!"

Her heart stuttered at the sound of her own name. She turned, eyes landing on a woman a few feet away who was balancing a toddler on one hip and adjusting the strap of a baby carrier slung across her chest.

It took a second, maybe two, before recognition struck.

Lucy McDonald.

Time had worn down the glossy edges of the girl Dylan used to call her best friend. Lucy's brown hair was pulled back in a messy bun, her T-shirt smudged with something suspiciously sticky, and dark circles clung beneath her eyes. She looked older, tired... but still unmistakably Lucy.

Their eyes met.

"Dylan?" Lucy's voice was tentative, almost disbelieving. "Is that really you?"

Dylan froze, her fingers tightening around the handle of her shopping basket.

Lucy smiled and shifted her weight, bouncing the toddler on her hip. "This is Dylan," she said, gesturing towards the boy clinging to her, who was now playing with her earring. "I named him after you."

Dylan blinked. "You... did?"

"Yeah." Lucy's expression softened. "You were such a big part of my life. Back then. I always thought... well, even after everything that happened, I wanted to remember the good parts."

Dylan's throat tightened. She stared at the child, her namesake, and then at the sleeping infant strapped to Lucy's chest. "Two kids?"

"Yeah," Lucy said with a soft laugh. "Liza's only four months. I'm officially outnumbered."

"I can see that," Dylan said, her voice a little too sharp, her emotions catching her off guard. There was so much she wanted to say. So much she wanted to ask. Why Lucy had turned away when she'd needed her most. Why no one had stood up for her back then.

Lucy seemed to sense the shift in her tone and cleared her throat. "Hey, um... I know it's been a long time, but maybe we could grab a coffee sometime? Catch up?"

Dylan hesitated. Her gut twisted, heart racing. She wanted to scream yes and no all at once. Instead, she forced a tight smile.

"Maybe. I, uh, I've got a bunch of things I have to take care of today." She took a step back. "But it was nice seeing you."

Lucy looked like she wanted to say more, but Dylan didn't wait. She turned and hurried towards the checkout lanes, the image of that little boy's smile haunting her as she tried to breathe through the sudden weight in her chest.

By the time she reached her car, she was trembling.

She didn't know what she was running from anymore—her past, her feelings, or the fact that, even after everything, a small part of her missed her old friend. Missed being part of this town.

But she wasn't ready to face any of it.

Not yet.

Chapter Eight

For the next few days, Abe worked with the horses from sunup to sundown. It was the kind of bone-deep exhaustion he welcomed—honest work, no cameras, no expectations beyond patience and grit. Just him, the salt in the air, and two damn stubborn horses.

Stormy had, after the third day, taken to the saddle like she'd been waiting for it all her life. She had a smooth gait, smart eyes, and a responsive nature that made riding her feel like a dance. He found himself smiling more when he was out with her, letting the miles stretch behind them as they galloped along the dunes and into the edges of the pine trails.

Blaze was another story. The gelding fought the bit like it had personally offended him. No wonder he'd been up for auction. Every ride was a tug-of-war with head tossing, feet stomping, and teeth flashing. Abe had the bruises to prove it. Still, he saw the fire in the horse's eyes, the kind that reminded him of himself when he'd first picked up a guitar with too much to say and no idea how to say it.

That morning, sweat dampened his shirt as he stepped

out of the round pen, brushing a hand down Blaze's neck while the horse huffed through his nose, then finally settling after he gave him a carrot. Abe led him back towards the paddock, letting the tension bleed from his muscles.

He didn't hear her at first over the distant waves or the wind that was blowing steadily from the cliffs. He smelled her soft perfume, springtime flowers, and turned. She was there, walking up from the path that led to the beach, the sun catching on her loose hair, the breeze tugging at the edges of her pale blue shirt.

Dylan.

She stopped at the fence, one hand resting on the top rail like she'd always belonged there.

"I saw you out here," she called. "Decided to come up and say hi."

He blinked, surprised by how fast his heart jumped at the sight of her. "You walked up here just to say hi?"

"Sure, why not?" Her smile was easy. "I was jogging on the beach." She motioned behind her. "Decided to take a detour."

He noticed then that she was wearing jogging shorts, the kind that flowed with her movements and looked soft like her skin. The tank top she wore matched her eyes and hair perfectly.

"Convenient detour," he teased, hitching Blaze's reins over the fence rail and walking over to her. "You missed a great show. Blaze nearly bit my ear off this morning," he said, wiping his hands on the towel slung over his shoulder.

Her eyes drifted towards the horse. "He looks like he's still plotting."

Abe laughed. "Oh, he is. I'm just winning for now."

She looked back at him, her gaze softer than he expected. "You look... different out here."

"Dirty?" he suggested.

She chuckled. "No. Relaxed. Like this is where you're supposed to be."

He leaned on the fence next to her. "Funny. I was just thinking the same thing about you. You look more relaxed than before. Settling back in?"

A flicker of something crossed her face—emotion, hesitation, maybe both—but she didn't look away. Instead, she just shrugged slightly.

Deciding not to spook her, he asked, "You want to meet them properly?" He nodded at the horses.

She hesitated, then gave a small nod. "Sure."

He opened the gate and held it for her and as she stepped through.

After a quick introduction, during which Stormy instantly nuzzled Dylan's shoulder, he led Blaze into the barn. Dylan followed behind with Stormy walking calmly beside her like they were already best friends. Abe watched them out of the corner of his eye, noting how natural Dylan looked next to the horse. Maybe not completely comfortable, but definitely not afraid.

"Just tie her there," he said, motioning to the cross ties. "I'll grab the brushes."

She clipped Stormy in place while he moved through the tack room, grabbing two sets of brushes and a couple of cooling cloths. When he returned, he handed her one without a word and started working Blaze down, sweeping the brush in long, even strokes along the gelding's sweaty coat.

They worked in quiet rhythm for a few moments, the sounds of the barn settling around them—horses shifting, birds chattering in the rafters, the distant crash of waves.

"You look like you've done this a time or two," he said over his shoulder.

"My dad was the town vet, remember?"

"Right." He smiled. "Did you have horses?"

"A Shetland pony and a few goats. We used to watch horses up at our place when needed. I remember having an old mare for an entire summer." Her smile was fast and genuine. "You have horses, right?"

He nodded. "Four of them. No goats." He smiled. "Yet."

She chuckled. "These two seem stubborn."

"I can do stubborn," he joked.

"Are yours broken in?"

"They are now. It took me five weeks to break Marty."

"I ran into an old friend yesterday," she said after a long pause.

Abe glanced up. She wasn't looking at him anymore, just focused on the brush as she worked over Stormy's back.

"Oh?"

"She named her son after me," she said, her voice soft. "I didn't expect that."

He leaned against Blaze, letting the gelding nibble at the salt block while he waited for her to go on.

"She asked me to grab some coffee." Dylan stopped brushing for a moment, her hand resting on the mare's side as her eyes watched dust motes floating in the sunlight. "I said no. Well... I didn't really say no. I mumbled something stupid and ran away."

Abe stayed quiet. Sometimes silence said more than words could.

She let out a long breath and picked up brushing again, slower this time. "I'm just not ready for that. For them. For... forgiveness, I guess. Or pretending like nothing happened back then."

"What did happen?" he asked gently.

She finally looked at him. "She turned her back on me when I needed her. When everyone else did too. I had..." She lifted her shoulders slightly. "I had no one."

His chest tightened at the vulnerability in her voice. She wasn't angry. Not really. Just hurt. And maybe a little lost.

"She looked tired. Worn down. I thought seeing her like that would make me feel something. Vindicated. I don't know. But she looked so tired. She had her little girl strapped to her chest, her son on her hip. She was pushing her groceries while her son, Dylan, hung onto her arms. And I felt..." Dylan trailed off and shook her head as she looked down at her fingers again. "Guilty. And sad. And angry. All at once."

Abe stepped away from Blaze and moved beside her. Close enough to feel her energy shift. "That's a lot to carry."

She gave a hollow laugh. "Story of my life."

"I think it's okay to walk away," he said. "And I think it's okay if one day you walk back, too. It doesn't have to be today or tomorrow, but maybe someday you'll be ready. I bet it took a lot of courage for her to let you see her like that. A lot more to invite you to coffee."

Dylan nodded slowly, the tension in her shoulders loosening as she looked at him again. Really looked. For the first time, Abe saw the walls drop. Just a little. But it was enough.

"Time doesn't heal all wounds, that saying is way off." He took her shoulders gently. "Letting things out, however you can, helps."

She took a deep breath. "I suppose your music is your release." She glanced back at the horses, not waiting for a response from him. "I used to spend a lot of time in barns with my dad. We'd talk." She locked eyes with him. "Being here, brings it all back."

He nodded, afraid that if he spoke, she'd close up again.

"I... didn't meant to unload on you." She rolled her shoulders, then surprised him by lifting up on her toes and brushing her lips across his. "Thanks for listening."

He stilled. Unable to move. The kiss had been light, casual. Yet, somehow, it felt so... powerful. Like a tsunami had hit him square in the chest, knocking out his breath and turning his world topsy-turvy.

"Dylan." His voice was low as he watched her still. Then he was pulling her close, covering her mouth with his. Her body melted into his instantly, her fingers slipping up to his hair, holding him tight.

In all of his years, he'd never felt anything so passionate. Whatever happened from this moment on, this mattered.

Then she stiffened in his hold and took a step back. She shook her head and chuckled nervously. "I didn't mean to come here and blather all over you."

"You didn't," he said, unsure of his own voice. He didn't want to say anything that would make her leave now. So, instead, he asked her if she'd help feed the horses and then join him for dinner.

After a moment, she nodded and they quickly finished brushing down the horses and then fed them, scooping oats and tossing hay. She stayed by his side, listening when he spoke about Blaze's progress and laughing when Stormy nuzzled her shoulder for treats.

As the sun started to dip lower over the Pacific, golden light streamed through the barn slats, soft and unhurried.

Abe watched her, something in her eyes shifting, opening.

This this was what he'd been hoping for.

She was finally letting him in.

They walked back to the house, and she sat in the kitchen, watching him and listening to him talk about his ranch, horses, and home while he cooked up some cast-iron-skillet fajitas, one of the few things he could make on a gas stove without screwing it up.

"I didn't know you could cook," she said, one brow raised, clearly impressed as she watched him slice peppers and onions like he actually knew what he was doing.

"Yeah, I don't really mention it in interviews," he joked. "I can only make a handful of meals without burning down the kitchen." He tossed the colorful strips into the hot pan, where they hissed on contact. "I can handle the basics. You live on the road long enough, you either learn to cook or you live off beef jerky and diner pie. Road trip food can only satisfy you for so long."

She chuckled, her arms crossed lightly over the table. "Road trip food isn't so bad."

"Spoken like someone who's never been stuck on a tour bus in the middle of Texas during a heatwave with nothing but a half-melted granola bar and a broken AC unit."

He flashed her a grin and caught the way she smiled back, soft, relaxed, unguarded. It hit him low and deep, how natural this felt. Her, sitting in his best friend's kitchen. Him, cooking like they'd done this a hundred times before.

As he plated the sizzling fajitas, she stood and grabbed the silverware and napkins without being asked. It took her a few times to find everything, but it was almost like she belonged there.

They sat across from each other at the table, sunlight slanting in through the window, painting golden lines across the wood grain.

"So," he said between bites, "when were you going to tell me you are a private investigator?"

She almost choked on the bite of food she'd taken. "I..." She shook her head. "How did you know?"

"It wasn't hard to find out." At first, it had pissed him off. He was used to people lying to him. He'd hoped that Dylan was different.

He really hoped she wasn't there for him, but something told him she was.

She stared at him, searching his face, probably trying to gauge just how pissed he was. But the truth was he wasn't. Not anymore. Not really. And not after that kiss. He was curious. Intrigued. But mad?

Not when she looked at him like that. Like maybe she hadn't expected kindness from him... and wasn't sure she knew what to do with it.

He dropped his voice a little. "You can ask me anything, Dylan. If you want answers, just ask."

For a long beat, she didn't say anything, just studied him in that quiet, intense way of hers.

And then, slowly, she set down her food and nodded. "Okay."

Abe took another bite, doing his best to act casual while every part of him felt like it was holding its breath.

Because that single word meant something.

It meant maybe. It meant not yet.

And most importantly...

It meant she wasn't running.

"Kara Sinclair." The name hung in the air like an iron fist to the gut.

He set his fork down slowly and took a sip of the cold soda.

"She was the woman I thought I was going to grow old

with," he answered truthfully. He'd never admitted that before.

Denial.

He'd been warned, threatened, and he'd sworn not to mention his closeness with Kara.

He watched her eyebrows rise slightly.

"Were you with her that night?"

"Earlier." He nodded. "That much is already out there in interviews."

She slowly nodded. "Were you driving?"

He sighed and leaned back in the chair. "No." His voice was laced with regret. "No." He closed his eyes. The violence of what had happened that night flashed behind his closed lids. "No," he said again, softer this time.

Dylan took his hand. The soft contact centered him a little. His eyes opened and locked with hers. "If I had been" —he shook his head—"she'd still be alive. I would have been taking her home, not the other way around."

"You can't do that to yourself," she said.

Abe gave a humorless laugh and stared down at their empty plates. "I know," he said. "But I do. Every day. Every night."

He stood and started clearing the dishes, mostly to have something to do with his hands. The weight of the conversation pressed hard on his chest, but the words kept coming steadily, like they'd been waiting for this moment to be spoken.

"She dropped me off around midnight," he said as he rinsed the plates. "I'd had too much to drink at dinner. She hadn't had anything, at least not that I'd seen. We argued before she left. Something stupid. Probably my ego. I had thought..." He glanced over his shoulder and changed tactics. "That much I'll own."

Dylan stood too, helping without a word, drying the dishes that he washed.

"She said she was going home. It was late, and she'd been quiet all night. Distant. I figured she just needed space. So I let her go." He shook his head, gripping the edge of the sink. "But she didn't go home. Not even close."

There was a long pause.

"She ended up five miles in the opposite direction of her home. Crashed into an underpass off Old Mill Road." His voice dropped to a whisper. "Her car was mangled. Totaled. But when the cops got there... she was in the passenger seat."

Dylan stopped drying and just looked at him. Something told him that she knew that bit of news already. Which surprised him.

Thanks to Tony, his PR manager, all of this, his connection to Kara, had been kept out of the press. His only connection had been highlighted in one small article, where they'd said that he and Kara had gone out a few times. Until the recent article had come out. That was the main reason he was hiding out in Pride.

"That part never made the reports. Everyone assumed she was driving. Why wouldn't they? It was her car. But she wasn't. Someone else was behind the wheel. And they're the reason she's gone." The anger flared like it always did when he thought about the unanswered questions. He turned around, his jaw tight. "Who was driving, Dylan? Because I don't know. I didn't see anyone else that night. I assumed she went straight home. But the direction she went, where the accident had occurred was in the opposite direction of her place. Plus, the timeline..." He ran a hand through his hair. "She should have been home hours before the crash. None of it adds up. I've hired my fair share of PIs in the past. The top of the top. No one could give me answers." He ran his hands through his hair, wanting to pull it out like he always did when he thought about that night. About Kara.

Dylan looked like she wanted to ask a dozen more questions but was trying to hold back.

"And the worst part?" he added. "Whoever was in that driver's seat... had walked away. The passenger side of the car had taken the brunt of the damaged. No one saw whoever had been driving. No one reported anything about the accident until almost half an hour.. Whoever had been driving, vanished with the damn fog that had been reported that night."

They stood in silence for a long moment, the only sound the hum of the fridge.

Finally, Dylan spoke. "You didn't kill her."

He looked up, meeting her gaze. It wasn't a question nor an accusation. It was more like reassurance. To whom though?

"I didn't think you could've," she said quietly. "But I think someone's gone to a lot of trouble to make sure no one ever finds out the truth," she added more slowly, as if she was choosing her words carefully.

Abe swallowed hard. "I've gone back over it a thousand times. Security footage from the townhouse I lived in at the time. Witnesses. Hell, I even broke into the impound lot one night just to look at her car myself." He gave a broken laugh. "And then, two weeks after the crash, someone torched it. Destroyed the whole lot."

Dylan's eyes widened. "That wasn't in the reports."

"Exactly." He stepped closer, his voice dropping. "Whoever's behind this has money. Power. Reach. And they've buried everything."

Dylan nodded slowly, her PI instincts clearly kicking in. "Then we dig it up."

He stared at her, that same quiet fire in her eyes.

This time, it was him who reached for her hand. "Are you sure?"

She nodded. "I have nothing else to do."

"Who hired you? Truthfully? Was it Kevin or her parents?"

She paused for a second, and he could tell she was going to give him the truth. "Kevin."

He shrugged. "You're not the first he's hired. You are, however, the first who managed to get close to me."

Her eyes darted away. "I..."

He stopped her by laying a finger over her lips. "I wouldn't be here if I didn't want to be close to you," he said, meaning it.

She gave him a weak smile.

His eyes narrowed slowly as he thought about it. "While we're speaking the truth." Her eyes moved up to his. "Someone broke in here the other night. The night of the wedding..."

Chapter Nine

Shit. Okay, yeah, she'd have to come clean.

"Abe," she started, but then his phone rang and he held up a finger as he pulled his cell from his back pocket. He sighed as he looked down at the name.

"Hey, Tony," She listened to his one-sided conversation. "No, yeah, okay, sure." Abe sighed. "Four weeks." He rolled his shoulders and walked over to the window. "No." There was a long pause. "No." He glanced over his shoulder and said no again before he hung up.

"Problems?" she asked, hoping the interruption would keep her from having to confess to breaking in.

"No," he said again. "Did you break in?"

She swallowed and then nodded.

"Why?" he asked, his eyes narrowing.

"I was working." She moved over and sat down, taking a sip of her soda. "Trying to find out more about Kara's death."

He sat across from her, soaking in what she had just admitted. He had to come to terms with the fact that she wasn't just some bystander who didn't know who he was like she'd pretended. She wasn't just a girl that he could have a summer fling with. She had lied to him.

"Kara's brother has always believed I had something more to do with that night." He frowned, avoiding her eyes. "He knows I didn't." He shook his head. "We were roommates for a while. That's how I met Kara."

Her eyebrows rose in shock. Not only was he not acting mad at her, he was giving her information she hadn't found anywhere. "He did not mention that piece of evidence, nor is it anywhere in the reports."

"No, I suppose he wouldn't. He was unofficially living with me for a few weeks back then. His name wasn't on the lease." He sighed and closed his eyes for a moment. "Why don't I walk you back to your car," he suggested, standing up.

Before she could argue, he took her hand and gently pulled her to her feet.

For a brief moment, she thought he was going to kiss her again, but then he took a step away.

They headed out into the fading light, the sound of the surf steady and calming as they crossed the grassy yard and descended the wooden stairs leading down to the beach. The air was cooler now, a salty breeze brushing over her skin as her shoes hit the sand.

For a while, they didn't speak, the only sounds between them the crunch of their footsteps and the distant call of gulls over the water. Dylan tucked her hands into her shorts pockets, eyes focused on the waves ahead as she collected her thoughts.

"I wasn't supposed to get emotionally involved," she said finally, breaking the silence. "Kevin hired me a few weeks back. He said he just wanted closure. Told me that the police had botched the investigation and that... things didn't add up. He suggested I start with you."

She glanced at Abe, who was listening silently beside her, his expression unreadable in the dim light.

"He didn't tell me about your history," she added. "Didn't mention he knew you at all, let alone that you'd been roommates."

Abe's jaw ticked, but he didn't speak.

"He was right about one thing, though," she continued. "The case was sloppy. Half of the files were incomplete, and any time I try to request official reports, I hit a brick wall. It feels like someone wants it buried." She paused. "And they've done a damned fine job of it too."

They crested a low dune, and her car came into view in the distance, parked beneath a light in the public parking lot.

"I wasn't looking to get this close to you," she added quietly. "At least not at first."

"But you found me anyway," he said softly.

She nodded, her throat tight. "I did."

Abe slowed a little, then turned towards her. "And now?"

She stopped walking, staring out over the darkening waves. "Now I want the truth. And I think the only way to find it is to work with you."

He nodded after a few beats, then stepped beside her again. "Then we'll find it."

She took his hand. "Something told me, from the start, that you weren't involved."

He took a deep breath and glanced up at the sliver of the moon. "I don't trust easily. Not after..." He shook his head and then turned back towards her. "I dropped my guard with you. Don't make me regret it."

She felt as if she'd been slapped. All she could do was give him a silent promise with a quick nod of her head.

"From here on out, I'll expect only the truth. You give it, and you'll get it." His eyes searched hers.

"That's fair," she whispered.

He swallowed and then took her hand, and they walked the rest of the way in silence, a different kind this time, one not filled with tension or suspicion but with something steadier. A quiet understanding. A fragile trust.

When they reached her car, she turned to him, her hand already on the door. "I'm not good at this either," she admitted. "The... trusting part."

Abe smiled gently, reaching out to brush a windblown strand of hair from her cheek. "Yeah. I figured as much"

For a moment, they just stood there, the ocean behind them, the sliver of a moon hanging high above them with all the stars.

This time, she let him make the move.

When he finally lowered his lips towards hers, she felt her entire body vibrate with desire. At least he hadn't kicked her out or, worse, called the police on her and had her hauled in for B&E.

When his mouth covered hers and she tasted him on her tongue, she relaxed and melted like she had during that first kiss.

This was something she'd never had before. Something she so desperately wanted to explore. To understand more deeply.

Then, without another word, he pulled away.

"Goodnight, Dylan," he said softly, and then he turned and started walking back down the beach.

She waited, watching until he was nothing more than a shadow before she got in her car and closed the door.

She sat there for a long moment, her fingers resting on the wheel, unmoving. Her lips still tingled, her chest was tight from the warmth of his kiss and the deeper weight of everything that had just passed between them. She drew in a breath, long and slow, trying to slow her racing thoughts.

This wasn't what she'd come here for.

And yet it was the only part of this town that felt real.

Why hadn't he turned her away the moment he'd found out who and what she was? The only answer she could come up with was that he was telling the truth. He wanted to find who was driving that night as badly as he'd said.

She'd felt that in her bones from the moment she'd started watching him. Really watching him.

Whatever had happened more than five years ago, Abe Collins had had nothing to do with the death of the woman he had loved.

And it was clear that he had loved Kara. If the look in his eyes in that faded photograph wasn't proof enough, the way his voice cracked when he spoke about her left no doubt.

The roads were quiet as she drove back towards her house. The porch lights throughout town flickered on as night fell fully over the coast, casting shadows over picket fences and gravel driveways. Everything about the town looked the same. But it wasn't. Not really. And neither was she.

Once inside the log cabin, she kicked off her running shoes by the door and made her way into her dad's small office at the back of the house. The room still smelled faintly of old paper and leather from her dad's years of use, and she found a strange comfort in that as she powered up her laptop.

Her inbox chimed the moment it connected to the Wi-Fi.

Kevin Sinclair.

She stared at the name for a second, debating whether to open it or not. But eventually she clicked.

Any updates? It's been over a week since you returned to Pride. I'm starting to get the sense you're holding something back. If you've found anything, even something small, you need to tell me. I'm not paying you to go dark. Call or email, your choice.

Dylan leaned back in her chair and stared at the screen, chewing her thumbnail. He wasn't wrong. She was holding back information from him. But she couldn't tell him that Abe knew who she was now. Not yet. Not when everything had shifted so completely in just a matter of hours.

Instead, she clicked reply and began to type.

I'm still digging. You were right about the inconsistencies in the report. I've found something that might be significant, but I need time to verify before jumping to conclusions.

Give me a couple more weeks. I promise, I'll have a full update for you then.

—Dylan

She stared at the message for a beat, then hit send before she could change her mind.

Leaning back, she exhaled and let her eyes drift closed. Abe had been honest with her. Brutally honest. And tonight, she had seen the obvious weight that he still carried about Kara in his grief, his questions, and his uncertainty about the past.

She had come to this town chasing the truth. But now, part of her wasn't sure what she'd do if the truth hurt someone she was starting to care about.

Shutting down her laptop, she stood, rubbing the

tension from the back of her neck. Whatever happened next, she'd have to be careful. Not just with what she found, but with whom she trusted. And most importantly, with what she was willing to lose in the process.

She needed ice cream. Walking over to the fridge, she pulled out some Ben and Jerry's and turned on the news. Halfway through the report, she switched to a crime movie and fell asleep on the sofa with an empty ice cream container on her lap and murder in her dreams.

The next morning, Dylan woke stiff and disoriented, one arm hanging off the sofa and an empty pint of Ben and Jerry's nestled between two throw pillows like a sad badge of honor. The crime movie had been replaced by some over-enthusiastic morning show host who looked far too cheerful for the hour. She groaned, sat up, and winced as her neck protested the night spent curled like a question mark.

After a quick shower and a fresh change of clothes, she grabbed her bag and headed into town. She needed caffeine, a moment of normalcy, and maybe, just maybe, a quiet place to think.

The Brew-Ha-Ha was buzzing with its usual charm. Eclectic music drifted from hidden speakers, the scent of roasted beans, cinnamon, and sugar wafted through the air, and the low murmur of voices could be heard over clinking mugs. Dylan stepped up to the counter and ordered a vanilla latte and a blueberry scone before sliding into one of the deep armchairs near the window with a worn paperback mystery.

She'd barely read two pages before a familiar voice startled her.

"Dylan?"

She looked up to see Lucy standing just a few feet away, her son clinging to her leg. Her newborn was asleep in the stroller. Today, Lucy looked less frazzled but still worn, like someone who hadn't had a full night's sleep in years. Her hair was swept up into a messy bun, and her oversized cardigan was speckled with what might've been cracker crumbs or glitter, maybe both.

Beside her stood a tall, solidly built man with kind eyes and a baby carrier slung over one arm.

"Troy, this is Dylan, the one I told you about." Lucy's voice was soft but edged with nervous excitement. "Dylan, my husband, Troy. He works at the Coast Guard facility." She sighed. "Can I... would you mind if I sat with you? Troy's going to take the kids to the park for a bit."

Dylan blinked, surprised but too polite to say no. "Uh, sure. Of course."

Troy gave her a small wave. "Nice to meet you." He bent to scoop Dylan, her namesake, into his arms and murmured something to Lucy before heading out the door without the stroller, holding his daughter and his son in his arms. He looked like an expert dad, not someone who had never cared for both kids before now.

Lucy eased down across from her, exhaling like someone who'd just run a marathon. "God, thank you. I love them, but sometimes I just need one hour without someone screaming or wiping their nose on my jeans."

Dylan smiled, though she could tell it didn't quite reach her eyes. "No problem."

They sat in silence for a moment, Lucy nursing her own latte before finally speaking again. "I've wanted to talk to you for years. I just didn't know if you'd want to hear it."

Dylan's fingers tightened slightly around her mug.

"I was scared," Lucy admitted, eyes fixed on the table. "Everything that happened... how everyone turned their backs on you, including me. I didn't want to dismiss our friendship, but I was a coward. After what I'd gone through, I just wanted... popularity," she blurted out the last word like she'd just ripped of a bandage.

Dylan didn't answer right away. The past had settled between them like fog—thick, unspoken, impossible to ignore.

"I named my son after you," Lucy added softly, "because deep down, I always knew that you didn't deserve any of it. I am so deeply sorry that I hurt you."

That nearly undid her. Dylan blinked hard, staring out the window so Lucy wouldn't see the shimmer in her eyes.

"You don't owe me anything," Lucy said, reaching across the table, not to touch, just to be closer. "But if you ever want to talk... or scream... or throw things, I'm around."

Dylan swallowed the knot in her throat. "Thanks," she managed. "I'm just... not there yet."

Lucy nodded like she understood. "I get it. When you are, I'll be here." She gave her a weak smile. Dylan nodded slightly in understanding.

They finished their drinks in silence, though it wasn't quite as strained as before. When Troy returned with the kids in tow, Lucy smiled and gave Dylan a hug that she didn't expect.

As Dylan walked back to her car, the warmth of the coffee and the weight of old wounds tugged at her chest. Lucy's words had cracked something open. Maybe, just maybe, not everything from the past had to stay broken.

But that didn't mean she was ready to forgive.

Not yet.

Chapter Ten

Finding a few things out about Dylan Roselyn Beck hadn't been too hard. He's started by asking around town about her. Everyone in Pride knew who she was and exactly what she had been doing for, well, her entire life.

From what he found out, young Dylan had been a loner who was bullied. Her mother had taken off shortly after her birth, leaving her and her father all alone. Her dad, who had been the town vet, had been almost forty years older than Dylan's mother, which had caused quite a stir in the small town. Dylan had apparently paid the price of all those rumors for most of her young childhood.

Everyone in town also mentioned the friendship between Dylan and Lucy McDonald, now Lucy Gilbert after she'd married Troy Gilbert, an engineer up at the Coast Guard base. They thought it was a shame that Lucy had treated Dylan the way she had, considering how close they'd been early on in school.

That could account for why Lucy had changed her life around after she had children of her own.

After graduation, Dylan left town and headed to Portland, where she worked for a small PI firm while going to college. Shortly after graduating, she'd started her own firm. She'd only returned to town for a few months last year to look after her dad until he passed.

There were other small bits and rumors, but nothing everyone could agree on.

Still, he felt as if he barely knew her at this point. When they'd been in the barn, she'd opened up to him for the first time and he had to admit, he desperately wanted it to happen again.

He'd guessed that it had been her who'd broken into the house after finding out what she did for a living. Besides, when he'd seen her run on the beach, he had recognized her as the person he'd seen running across the dark field. When she'd confirmed it, he wasn't mad. Oddly. She hadn't disturbed anything and, after finding out that her main goal was to find out what had happened to Kara, how could he be mad? After all, he had been desperate for answers for years himself.

After he'd walked Dylan to her car the night before, he'd tried to muster up some anger towards her the whole way home. But none came. Instead, an eagerness to work with her had sprung up. The excitement about possibly solving the riddle that had torn his heart apart all those years ago had him flying high.

More importantly, the thrill of seeing her again outweighed any anger. The fact that Dylan had made his broken heart beat rapidly for the first time since Kara tickled the back of his mind.

The next morning, he rose before the sun, while the sky was still bruised in shades of deep navy and violet. He pulled on a sweatshirt to ward off the salty morning chill, grabbed his worn notebook and guitar case, and made the slow trek up the spiral stairs of the lighthouse. He'd wanted to watch the sunrise from up there from the moment he'd seen the place and figured it was the perfect spot to write what he'd been feeling for the past few days.

The salty breeze bit at his skin as he stepped out from behind the protective glass walls. The view at the top, miles of ocean stretching in every direction, made it worth every step.

He sat down on the chair he'd dragged outside and, with the ocean to the right and the rising sun to his left, settled down. After tuning the guitar, he closed his eyes and took a deep breath.

While the first sliver of light broke the horizon, he strummed his guitar and started playing a new melody that had been circling in his subconscious.

The lyrics came slowly at first.

A woman made of shadows and smoke,
   with eyes that promise, but words that lie.
   Her lips are like wine, shakes me like thunder.
   Will she ever truly be mine.

Mystery woman,
   Questions and riddles,
   She's a midnight flame in a world gone cold,
   Slipping through fingers I thought could hold.
   Every kiss burns, every glance deceives,
   But I chase her still, 'cause I need to believe.
   Oh, mystery woman, don't disappear,
   Tell me your truth or whisper your fears.

. . .

He stopped occasionally, writing down each line. He didn't think too hard, just let everything flow out of him.

Dylan. She was everywhere in this song. In the longing, the uncertainty. In the ache behind each word.

You came to town with stories stitched,
  A smile rehearsed, the truth bewitched.
  But every secret that you keep
  builds a wall too high, a silence too deep.

She's a midnight flame in a world gone cold,
  Slipping through fingers I thought could hold.
  Every kiss burns, every glance deceives,
  But I chase her still, 'cause I need to believe.
  Oh, mystery woman, don't disappear,
  Tell me your truth or whisper your fear.
  She's a midnight flame in a world gone cold,
  Slipping through fingers I thought could hold.
  Every kiss burns, every glance deceives,
  But I chase her still, 'cause I need to believe.
  Oh, mystery woman, don't disappear,
  Tell me your truth or whisper your fear.

When he finally looked up, the sun had fully broken over the hills and trees, spilling molten gold across the waves of the Pacific. He closed the notebook and leaned back with a sigh, playing his new song, her song, one last time from memory. He let the song echo in his chest as he watched the world wake in front of him.

He didn't know what to do with it yet. But it was hers. All of it.

He made his way down from the lighthouse and cleaned up, then grabbed a hot mug of coffee. He drove into town to clear his head. He wasn't planning to stop at the bookstore but figured he'd browse the new releases for something exciting to read later that evening.

The bell over the door chimed, and the scent of aged paper and cinnamon hit him like a memory. How many days had he spent in the bookstore his mother had worked in most of her life? Too many to remember.

She'd been the reason he lost himself in pages. The reason it was so easy for him to twist words into songs. She'd never known how successful he had become, having died a year before Kara had.

While Kara's death haunted him with all the unanswered questions, his mother's hadn't been so complicated. Heart failure due to the medications she'd been on all her life while she'd waited for a transplant. Death had been a known possibility. She should have never had him. His birth had weakened the already frail body she'd been born with.

Still, they had been lucky to have as much time together as they had, and he was so thankful for every moment he'd had with such an amazing soul.

When he stepped inside the book store now, his eyes took a few seconds to focus in the darker room.

And then he saw her.

Dylan was sitting in the corner booth by the café section, laughing. Her long hair lay across her shoulders in two braids, and her sunglasses sat on top of her head as if she'd pushed them up and had forgotten them.

She had on a white and blue striped shirt with white shorts that showcased her long, tan legs, and his heart skipped several beats. She looked like a sun goddess. Tan. Toned. Happy.

Then he noticed that she was sitting with Nate Elliott, Juliette's brother. He'd met the man at Max and Juliette's rehearsal dinner.

He seemed like a good guy, but Abe wanted to march over there and... Well, the way that Nate was currently looking at Dylan, like he had all the time in the world and never wanted to leave, made his primordial instincts kick in. The man's sandy hair was tousled just enough to look styled, and he was smiling at Dylan like she was dessert.

Abe stood frozen in the doorway, debating what to do. Then someone entered behind him and he was forced to move inside. Without thinking, he moved towards a magazine rack and hid behind it and pretended to browse while he spied on the couple.

Nate leaned in and said something that had Dylan smiling behind the rim of her coffee mug. It wasn't the same smile that she gave him. It was lighter, almost... guarded. He frowned. Still, it twisted something low in his gut.

Abe didn't like the way Dylan's eyes sparkled when she laughed at one of Nate's jokes. And from the looks of it, the man was a very funny guy. He ground his back teeth.

Then the man leaned closer and flicked the back of a finger across Dylan's chin and Abe's vision almost grayed.

Needing a moment, he turned towards a display of new release books, grabbed one that he'd already read, and took a steadying breath as he hid behind the cover.

He wasn't going to walk over there and make a fool of himself, he told himself several times. He wasn't that guy. Not anymore.

But dammit, she could at least look like she remembered that she had kissed him yesterday and rocked his world. Like the night had meant something.

Instead, she looked like she was shopping for someone else to wreak havoc on.

He glanced over and noticed how well she fit into this little town, where people smiled and flirted and didn't carry around the weight of death, lies, or investigations. Or worse, the Hollywood elite, with their snobby parties and flashing cameras.

Abe put the book back and turned towards the exit, his jaw tight, his stomach sinking. He would never fit in here, just like he didn't fit in the elite LA circles. Sure, he could fake it, but he belonged on his ranch, alone with his horses.

He didn't know what Dylan was doing with Nate. Maybe there was nothing between the pair? Maybe she just liked bookstores and spending time with a guy who flirted and could make her laugh?

But as the bell chimed again behind him and the door closed, he realized he didn't want to lose his heart to a woman that had lied to get him.

"Hey." He turned around a few steps from the bookstore as Dylan rushed after him and reached for his arm. "What's the rush?" she asked, falling in step with him easily.

He glanced over his shoulder. "No rush, just... three's a crowd."

She glanced back and then laughed. "Nate flirts with everyone. With all women, all walks of life. He lays it on thick all the time. Trust me, he's harmless. Well, maybe." She shrugged and then laughed, then her smile grew. God, why did just seeing that smile cause his knees to grow weak.

"Were you jealous? Honestly, he's like a brother, if I had ever had one."

He shrugged and then surprised her by taking her hand, locking their fingers as they walked down the sidewalk towards the park in the center of town.

"Maybe," he admitted. They walked for a while in silence.

"So much has changed in town," she said when they reached the gazebo in the center of the town square. "Some things haven't."

"It must have been nice," he said, stopping and leaning on the railing and looking out over the green grass, the many colored flowers, and the families enjoying the summer day. "Growing up here."

"It had its moments." She leaned next to him. "Where did you grow up?"

He tilted his head. "Didn't you read that in my file?"

She shrugged. "You tell me."

He smiled. "Just outside of San Fran," he answered.

"City boy turned music star turned cowboy," she teased and had him laughing.

"Something like that."

"Siblings?"

He shook his head. "You?"

She shook her head. "Parents?"

He shook his head a little slower. "Dad died in a car crash when I was ten. Mom passed four years, six months, and..."—he calculated quickly— "four days ago."

She touched his arm lightly. "How long was she sick?" When he raised his eyebrows, she shrugged and reminded him, "It was in your file."

"Right." He motioned towards a bench under a tree. "Let's

sit in the shade." When she nodded, he took her hand again and they strolled over to sit before he answered her. "Mom was sick all her life, it seems. She claimed that she had been just as bad before I came along, but something always told me that was a lie." He leaned back and lifted an arm to wrap behind her shoulders and played with the ends of her braids.

He glance out and watched as Nate left the bookstore and headed across the street. He knew it was petty of him, but just in case the man glanced over, he shifted even closer to Dylan. "After a particularly bad flu the year before her death, things turned worse." The closeness of Dylan somehow made the pain of the loss sting less.

"My dad got pneumonia a few months before he went. I came home to watch over him." He saw her eyes turn sad and shifted slightly towards her, wanting to comfort her. He knew how it felt.

"There isn't a day that goes by that I don't wish I could pick up the phone and talk to her." He sighed. She frowned and glanced away.

He stopped playing with the ends of her hair.

"I... when I went away for college, I..." She shook her head. "I was too busy for calls."

He nudged her. "You were there when he needed you most."

She turned and met his gaze, and he forgot all about making another man jealous. Instead, his entire mind and body focused on her. Just her. How the light made her hair shine and warmed her skin, turning it a light pink. Her eyes almost glowed.

He was falling hard and fast for her, even though he knew deep down that he couldn't fully trust her. She still carried secrets. Deep down, she was hiding something else from him. What? Why? When would she trust him enough to open fully for him?

Her eyes seemed to be searching his as if looking for answers herself. Did she think he was hiding things from her? Did she really believe him when he told her he had nothing to do with Kara's death?

She moved ever so slightly towards him. Maybe it was in his mind? Maybe it was nothing more than a breeze blowing her towards him. Either way, when she was nothing more than a breath from him, he knew that he was lying to himself.

He was no longer falling in love with Dylan. No. That moment had come and gone in the blink of an eye. Abe Collins was one-hundred-percent already in full-blown love with Dylan Beck. And he had only kissed her twice.

Now, all that was left was to seal his fate with a kiss.

"Dylan," he whispered, but then someone called her name and Dylan blinked, breaking the moment.

Chapter Eleven

What in the hell was that? Dylan kept asking herself as she paced in the living room shortly after sunset. What. In. The. Hell!

Her entire body had... What? Been hijacked? Body. Mind. Heart. Soul. She'd almost sunk directly into him.

The scary thing was, she would have willingly gone.

She'd never felt anything like it before. Staring into Abe's eyes was like... well, circling a black hole. No one and nothing could stop her from being sucked in, completely.

After they had been interrupted, he'd listened to their conversation for a moment before she'd made excuses and had made a fast getaway, leaving Abe to head back towards the bookstore while she snuck away towards her car.

When she arrived back to her car, there was a new message on her phone from Kevin, who wanted to meet in an hour at his motel in Edgeview.

Why in the hell was he in Edgeview? When she tried to call him, she got his voicemail. She left him a few text messages but didn't receive a reply.

So she drove the thirty minutes to Edgeview and

knocked on his hotel room door for almost half an hour. Then she sent him three more messages and tried to call him a half dozen times with no luck. So she left him a message telling him that she had to get back to Pride and to call her when he could.

From what she knew about the man, he was a flake. He often missed important meetings, getting fired from job after job. It was only thanks to his family's wealth and power that he had any money to live on. But they were rolling in it, so Kevin's life was posh.

Since she was in Edgeview, she hit the larger grocery store for some necessities. She groaned when she spotted Tommy. He saw her and made a beeline towards her across the meat section. Fitting.

"There you are," Tommy said with a grin. He tried to wrap his arm around her shoulder, which she easily ducked. Placing her cart between their bodies, she pasted on a grin.

"Tommy." She was pleased when his eyes narrowed at her use of his old name.

"Tom." He laughed. "Remember?" His eyes turned mean, and she figured it wouldn't be long before she would see the real man behind his fake charm. "I was about to head out and meet up with some buddies at a club in town. Why don't you—"

"No, thank you." She tried to sidestep him again.

"Oh, come on, Dylan. You can't still be holding a grudge for putting cream cheese in your locker all those years ago. It was a silly childhood prank."

Her eyebrows arched. "Well, until now I had no idea who had done that, so no, I haven't been holding a grudge against you."

This time she was successful in getting away from him and losing him somewhere in the deli section. She finished her shopping and headed back to Pride without running into Tommy again or hearing from Kevin.

Back at home, she paced, frustrated at having wasted her entire evening.

Abe had left her body wanting, while her mind swirled about why Kevin hadn't shown and why he wasn't answering her messages. Not to mention she was now pissed at Tommy for the prank all those years ago.

She felt like punching something or someone.

She was just about to sit down at her computer and send Kevin an email when there was a knock on her door.

She assumed it was Kevin, but when she opened the door, she saw Abe. The porch light cast a bright glow over his broad shoulders and shadowed jaw, making him look more like trouble than any man had a right to.

"Hey," Abe said, his voice softer than she expected. "You left in a bit of a hurry."

She stepped aside, letting him in without thinking. "Yeah... I wasn't feeling great." Not technically a lie since her nerves were still rattled.

He stepped inside, glancing around like he was making sure she was alone. She expected him to keep questioning her fast escape or read too much into it, but he just looked at the bags on her counter.

"Need help putting those away?"

She gave a small shrug, grateful for the shift in attention. "Sure."

"Edgeview Market?" he asked, seeing the bag.

"They have the cereal and frozen meals I like," she said quickly. That wasn't a lie either, just not the whole truth of why she'd gone to town.

He rolled up his sleeves and started unpacking things, glancing in a few cupboards and then moving quickly.

God, he made the large kitchen feel small.

She watched him for a second, then shook off the lingering tension and joined him. The quiet between them was oddly comforting. No need to fill it with useless chatter. Just the rustle of bags, the opening of cabinets, the unspoken ease between them.

"You have a nice piece of property up here," he said, and she got the hint that he was trying to keep the conversation casual.

"Twenty acres," she said. "Half of it is hillside, but still..."

"Did I see a barn to the side?"

"Yes, that's where we kept our animals and any my dad was boarding temporarily. It's big enough for ten horses."

He whistled. "My ranch in Cali only has six stalls. I'm thinking of adding more. After working with Stormy and Blaze, I really want to get my hands on a few more to work with."

"You have four now, right?"

"Yeah, but," he started and then sighed. "They're all broken in."

"Bored?" she asked as he handed her the last box of crackers. She put them in the pantry.

"Desperately," he admitted, and she chuckled.

Abe leaned against the counter, arms crossed, and ran his eyes over her. Instantly, she could tell he was debating asking her something. It didn't take a PI to see the questions behind his gaze.

"You up for dinner?" he asked instead of whatever was on his mind.

"Yeah," she said after a moment. "Since my pantry is stocked, how about you help me cook something?"

His grin spread slowly, wickedly. "Tell me how to help."

Fifteen minutes later, the kitchen was filled with the scent of sautéing vegetables, grilled chicken, and warm spices. Dylan stirred the rice and chicken while Abe manned the cutting board.

"I came over here to discuss Kara's case..." he said without looking over at her.

She paused and wiped her hands on a dish towel. "Right." She sighed. Of course he'd come here to talk about the case. Why not jump right in then? "I've been going through my notes since we spoke last, along with the police files I could find. A few of the witness statement just don't sit right. There's just something..." She dropped off.

She kept her expression neutral. But when she thought of the missed meeting with Kevin, a jolt went through her.

"What kind of something?" he asked.

"Something about Kevin's statement that next morning. The timeline he mentions is fuzzy," she explained. "It's almost... too clean. Too planned. He knew the time down to the minute. Your statement reads like someone who is in shock. You couldn't remember the exact time Kara dropped you off. You knew where you'd eaten and that she had driven you home and dropped you off, and even that it had been slightly raining that night. His statement is more calculated. Like he was very careful or as if he planned it all out before answering every question. And it's odd that he practically vanished for a few years four months after his sister's death before resurfacing only two months ago. Three days before hiring me. You mentioned he'd hired a few other PIs over the years, but I can't find anyone or any agency that worked with him. Plus, I can't find anything on where he was for those years or even why he moved to Portland. He has no job. No permanent residence. He lives off his parents' money." Dylan stirred a little harder than necessary as she talked. "I mean, I guess people disappear all the time after the death of a loved one. It doesn't really mean anything, I don't think. But... it's bugging me."

"True," Abe said, giving her a quick look. "For weeks after Kara's death, Kevin was all over me and hounding the police, demanding that the accident be investigated while their parents were just grieving. When he stopped and moved away, I didn't hear where he'd gone, only..." He stopped talking and she glanced over at him. He frowned down at the cutting board. "I suppose I was just happy that he'd stopped hassling me and demanding that the police arrest me. He was crazed at times." He shook his head. "Their parents were not and seemed embarrassed at his actions."

"He had just lost his sister," she pointed out.

"And I lost..." He stopped abruptly and closed his eyes.

When she glanced at him, he was looking out the window into the darkness. "I wanted answers just as badly as he did. I still do." He walked over to dump the carrots into the pot.

"Any idea what he's doing back or what he's doing in Portland?" Abe asked, eyes fixed on hers.

She shook her head a little too quickly. "No clue."

Another half-truth. She wasn't ready to tell Abe about the meeting in Edgeview. Besides, it hadn't amounted to anything, Kevin hadn't even shown. Why stir up questions until she had answers?

Abe nodded, accepting it without pressing. "Now we've got you digging deeper. Hopefully, we will know more soon."

Still, when she looked at Abe, a flicker of guilt twisted in her stomach. She wasn't lying to him. Not really. Just... protecting him from a thread that hadn't unraveled yet.

But she knew that secrets had a way of pulling everything apart. And soon, hers might do just that. Maybe she was secretly sabotaging whatever was between them? After all, she'd gone her entire life believing she didn't deserve happiness.

"I didn't just come here for dinner," he surprised her by admitting. He reached over and turned off the gas stove, leaving the chicken, veggies, and rice simmering in the pan.

She set the spoon down. "No?" Her eyes scanned his and instantly heated when she saw the desire in his. His gaze dipped to her lips quickly and then back up.

"No." He sighed. "There are... things we need to discuss."

"Okay," she said slowly.

"First..." He cupped the back of her head, and moved slowly towards her. The kiss was light but hotter than the gas burner. Her mind stopped working as her desires took over her body. She leaned into him while his hands gripped her hips and his fingers fisted in her shirt.

"I wanted to do that earlier," he admitted as he rested his forehead against hers. "Now maybe I can think a little more clearly."

"Now I can't," she said with a chuckle.

"Today, earlier..." He leaned back a little more and searched her eyes. "I didn't mean to be an ass about Nate."

She smiled. "Dealing with jealousy isn't really my forte. I can honestly say that I've never had anyone experience that emotion because of me before."

"Well, now you can pin that merit badge on." He sighed. "I like kissing you. I hope soon we can do more, but..." He shook his head slightly. "We need to get some things out in the open first. We both need answers to questions that are blocking us like a brick wall."

She nodded slowly. "Trust isn't something that comes easily."

His eyes narrowed slightly as he dipped his head slightly in agreement.

"How about we eat?" she suggested after a heartbeat. "Then I can show you what I have gathered on this case."

His eyebrows arched. "You'd do that? Share with me? A suspect?"

She smiled. "I removed you from the suspect list the moment I heard you sing Kara's song at the wedding."

He frowned and closed his eyes. "No one else knows that I wrote it for her."

"No one else has to know." She touched his cheek and placed another kiss on his lips. "Now, why don't you grab us some beers while I dish us up food?"

They ate in the little dining area off the kitchen while she showed him the files that she had typed up on her laptop. She held back the full police report along with some of the images of the car and Kara at the scene of the accident. She did, however, go over one eye witness statement, an older man who had been out walking his dog. They also went over his and Kevin's statements, which were taken the morning after the accident.

There were no reports from a coroner. There were no more photos of Kara's body, other than the one of her still in the car. There was no investigative report on the vehicle or the tire marks on the road.

The old man had heard the accident and rushed to the scene. He said he'd seen a man with a build that matched both Abe's and Kevin's perfectly, running away from the accident.

This is, no doubt, why Abe and Kevin were questioned the next morning. But since Abe's roommate at the time remembered Kara dropping him off around nine-thirty, almost an hour before Kara's car hit the cement wall under the bridge, he was taken off the suspect list.

"Is this normal for a case?" he asked, averting his gaze from the image of Kara's wrecked vehicle sitting sideways in the ditch. It was the one image she was willing to show him. "The lack of... well, there just seems like there should be more here."

"There should be more reports from the coroner, the impound lot, and even forensics. Kara had her seatbelt on and was strapped into the passenger seat. Not the driver's side. Yet the police reports indicate that she was the driver and they suspected ice on the road to be a factor in the accident."

"Ice?" He frowned and leaned closer. "But the accident was in late August. There had been some rain earlier in the evening, during dinner and when she dropped me off at home, but it stopped shortly after, before her accident. There would have been no sleet or snow."

She nodded. "Yes, and all the weather reports show that the high temperature for that day had been seventy-two degrees Fahrenheit. The low for that evening was fifty-four."

He leaned back in his chair and closed his eyes. "She was wearing jean shorts and a T-shirt that evening. Her shirt had little blue flowers on it." His voice was low, soft, like he was pulling the memory from deep down. No doubt he could see her perfectly behind his closed eyes. "Her hair was braided in one long thick braid." His eyes opened and he ran his eyes over Dylan's darker hair, which she'd braided in two longer braids earlier that morning.

The pain behind his eyes made her swallow hard. She could remember just how her father looked that last day.

What he'd worn. Every word he'd said to her. The pain of the loss caused her chest to ache between her ribs, and she reached out and squeezed his hand lightly.

"Not a day goes by that I don't replay that last night we had together," he said, and she nodded in understanding. "Which is why, I suppose, you are here. I don't blame Kevin for wanting answers. I've wanted them too." He took a deep breath. "What's next? How do we get those answers?"

She thought a moment. "First step, since I have your full cooperation, is for you to answer more questions."

He nodded and rolled his shoulders. "Okay, I'm ready."

She shifted and sighed. "I'm not. To be honest, it's been a very long day." She glanced at her clock and winced at the late hour.

He did the same and sighed. "I have a meeting with my producer, James, and my PR manager, Tony, in the morning." He groaned. "Will late afternoon tomorrow work for you?"

"Yes." She nodded, not wanting to tell him that her schedule was wide open. Hell, the only reason she was in Pride was to get close to him.

When he stood up, she followed and was surprised when he started carrying their empty dishes back into the kitchen.

"I've got this," she said when he turned on the sink water. He glanced over his shoulder at her and her heart skipped several beats.

"One thing that my mother taught me that stuck was to always clean up when someone else does the cooking." He motioned beside him. "You can dry."

While they worked on the dishes together, they talked about his music. She was pretty sure he had hit a wall with talking about Kara and that night she died. There had been moments after her father's death that she hadn't wanted to talk about it or her feelings either. That was one of the reasons she'd hightailed it out of Pride quickly after the services.

When the last dish was dry and had been put away, she handed him the towel to dry his hands. Instead of taking it, he stepped closer to her and wrapped his arms around her.

"I don't want you to think that I only came here for... answers." His hands moved to her hips while his eyes landed on her lips. "I've been thinking about kissing you again."

She felt her knees almost buckle. If he hadn't been holding her, she might have just melted to the floor. God, why did he smell so sexy? He should smell like dish soap. Instead, there was a deep musky scent that surrounded him like a hug, and she wanted to be engulfed in it.

"Why think much longer?" she whispered, unwilling or unable to trust her own voice.

When his head bent down and his lips brushed hers, she melted against him. He tasted better than he smelled. The feel of his hard chest against her had her heart beat tripling.

When his tongue dipped in and trailed against hers, a soft moan started in her chest and escaped as he cupped her head so he could tilt it slightly.

She was putty in his hands. At that moment, she would have done anything to keep him from leaving.

He moved slowly, almost as if she were dessert and he was lapping her up and enjoying every lick. God, just the thought of him doing what he was doing to her mouth to the rest of her body had everything vibrating for him.

"Dylan," he sighed against her mouth. "I want to stay..."

"Stay," she begged, without giving him a heartbeat to

decide. Her fingernails dug into his arms, wishing to hold him closer.

His eyes met hers and she could see that he wouldn't. Not yet. She guessed he wouldn't until she found some answers. Anything.

Her heart slammed back down to reality and she took a step back, missing the feeling of him and the taste of him so much she swayed.

"I'll see you tomorrow," he said and, without saying goodbye, he walked out of her house, leaving her body wanting more than it ever had for that sweetest release.

Damn him.

Chapter Twelve

"The very last day for you to get me the lyrics for your music video is Tuesday," James Lyle reminded him.

"I can have them to you by then," he agreed, rubbing his forehead. He loved writing, singing, recording, and performing. What he hated was the technical aspect of his career. Meetings, promotions, filming videos, and of course, all the events where he had to kiss ass.

"Great. Are you sure you can't head into the studio before Max returns?" James asked again.

Abe held in a sigh.

"Three more weeks," he said. "Then I'll head straight into the studio for however long it takes."

"But you are still attending Friday night's gala?" James asked. "I have everything arranged for you. I'll send you the flight info and I've already booked your usual suite. Plus, there will be a car ready to take you to the party."

"Yes, I'll be there." He tried to hold in a groan. He didn't really want to go to the industry party that weekend. Sure, it was just one night, but that would be one night away from here and away from Dylan. Then he smiled. "Add a plus one for me."

James was quiet for a moment. "Is there something I should know?"

From the moment he'd signed his first contract with James, the man had seen to his every need.

"No," he answered and quickly asked, "How are Reba and Mason doing?" hoping to change the subject to the man's wife and one-year-old son.

He and James had been friends long before he'd signed his first record deal. Reba and Kara had been best friends, having met in college, and James and Reba had gotten together thanks to that connection. Two months after meeting, they'd tied the knot in a lavish wedding that had been in all the tabloids, thanks to Reba's family's power and James's hot career.

"Good," James said quickly. "Rumors have it you've been seen with a pretty auburn-haired woman up there? Is she the plus one? Are things getting serious?"

"No," he answered, slightly frustrated that James couldn't move on. Especially since Tony Carson, his PR manager, was on the line with them. Tony would try and use the relationship with Dylan to boost his next album, if he thought it was serious. After all, nothing sells music as well as the rumor of a budding romance. Well, nothing but heartbreak, at any rate. "Dylan and I are just... figuring things out."

"Dylan?" He could practically hear James frown through the line.

"She's just a new friend," he added quickly, "and off limits."

"Leave the man alone," Tony broke in. "If he says it's off limits, let's respect that decision."

Tony had always been on every call James and he had. After a little snafu a year ago, when someone had leaked details about his relationship with Kara. He figured both men wanted to watch his back.

James had a one-year-old and was no doubt sleep deprived, which is probably why he was quiet most of the call.

At this point, by Tony's thinking, coming clean about his and Kara's relationship and exposing his heartbreak about her death might boosted sales for his next album.

Especially his new song "Lost in the Dark," a song that he'd written for Kara.

James wasn't too keen on the idea. Abe no longer cared at this point. The truth was bound to get out sooner or later.

But this time, what he had with Dylan, it was different. He didn't want what he felt for her to be a tool to sell more records.

Abe's fingers curled into a fist on the arm of his chair. "Dylan Beck is not to be used as a PR stunt," he said clearly, each word clipped, cold, for the benefit of both men.

The silence that followed was tight.

Finally, James cleared his throat. "Of course not. Just covering all angles."

"Now, if you don't mind, I have other business to get to," Abe said, rubbing his forehead again. The dull throb there had grown into a full-on pulse. He leaned back in the chair, the leather creaking under his weight. The thought of the cold turkey sandwich waiting in his fridge filled him with more irritation than hunger. He really ought to get some of those pre-made meals at the store. He was tired of cooking. Tired of... well, everything at the moment.

"One last thing," Tony broke in. "I've got a handful of new advertising opportunities. I'll email you later today.

Make your choices. Let me know. All of them are good and will help with your new album. Also, I'm working on your next tour and will let you know dates and venues."

"Thanks," Abe said flatly, already reaching for the button to end the call. "See you on Friday." He didn't wait for their goodbyes.

The moment the call ended, he pushed to his feet and stretched his arms above his head until his spine popped. The walls of the room felt smaller after that two-hour conversation, the air stale with the scent of leather, electronics, and ego. He needed space. Something real. Something alive.

Outside, the salty breeze hit him like a balm. He tugged on his boots and made the short walk to the barn. The moment he slid the doors open, he felt his tension ease.

The barn smelled of hay, saddle oil, and horse. Comforting, grounding, unlike the artificial tones and scripted nonsense from his call. Blaze poked his head over the stall gate and let out a soft whinny.

"Hey, boy." He reached out, scratching behind the gelding's ear as Blaze nuzzled into his palm, searching for a treat.

"Sorry, bud. Fresh out." He smiled faintly and patted the horse's neck. "Next time, I swear."

He moved through the barn, checking water levels and tossing extra hay into the stalls. Each familiar motion pulled him further away from the call, from James and Tony and the weight of their expectations.

He loved his music, loved writing it, playing it, performing it and, of course, the money that flooded in because of it. What he hated was the industry behind it. The fake smiles and people who wanted things from him and were always poking their noses into his personal life. Not that there had been much of that after Kara. Still, for the past few years, the media had tried to tie him to many women.

Some had been just friends. There were others he'd tried to get close to until they'd tried to use him to boost their own budding acting or modeling careers. He was tired of being used.

Then he thought of Dylan. Technically, she hadn't used him. Sure, she had played it cool to get close to him. For a reason. Not a selfish one, but... business? Looking into her eyes, he could tell she wanted answers about Kara's death as much as he did.

Since their cause was the same, he was willing to overlook her omissions the first few times they'd met. She was being honest with him now, that much was true. After all, everyone in town knew everything about her.

He'd overheard a story about her first date and how she'd been tricked into going out with a boy who had ditched her at the dance. Her entire class had been in on it. Even Lucy.

He thought about the conversation she'd had with him in the barn. The pain in her voice had been real when she'd spoken about her friend's betrayal. He didn't know what he'd do if any of his close friends ever turned on him like that.

As he stepped outside, the wind tugged at his shirt, stronger than it had since he'd been there. Like a storm was coming. He could almost smell it in the air coming off the Pacific.

He followed the narrow trail behind the stables, the well-worn path curving between the dune grass. When he reached the top of the ridge, he paused, the roar of the ocean filling his ears like a low, endless song. Closing his eyes for a moment, he just listened to it.

When he opened his eyes, he spotted a lone figure moving along the shore below, jogging at the edge of the foam. Tall. Athletic. Comfortable in his skin in the way Abe sometimes forgot how to be.

Nate Elliott. The man Abe had seen chatting with Dylan in the bookstore. The man who had been too friendly. Dylan had assured him there was nothing between them. But would Nate agree?

His jaw tightened slightly before he could stop it.

Nate's pace slowed as he approached the stairs. He looked up and spotted Abe at the top and raised a hand with an easy, genuine smile.

"Hey!" Nate called, jogging the last few steps to the base of the stairs. "Didn't think I'd run into you out here today."

Abe nodded and descended a few steps to meet him halfway. "Nice day for a run."

"It's not the best time of day, honestly. Mornings are more my game. Unfortunately, this morning I was working." Nate lifted the hem of his shirt to wipe his forehead. His abs flashed in the sunlight, and Abe instantly hated himself for noticing. "But at least it's nice and quiet, if not a little too hot."

Abe leaned against the wooden railing, forcing himself to relax. "You work at the Brew-Ha-Ha?"

"My family owns it. I've been working there for as long as I can remember. Now that Juliette is too busy and my folks have decided they want to travel more, I've stepped up to take over." Nate laughed. "Honestly, I never pictured myself wanting to return home. But Pride has a way of pulling you back in."

Abe let out a low chuckle despite himself. "Yeah, I've heard that more than once since I've been here."

"It's really a great place. Wonderful people." Nate stretched a calf muscle against the step, then he looked up again. "How are things up there?" He motioned to the buildings behind him.

"Good. Max and your sister's new horses, Stormy and Blaze, are getting settled in."

"Good. I still can't believe my sister has horses again." He shook his head. "Dylan mentioned the other day that you were breaking them in?"

There it was again. That uncomfortable twist low in his gut. A spark of something he didn't want to name, because he knew what it was. Jealousy. Ugly and sharp.

"Yes," Abe replied, schooling his voice into neutrality. "I have had horses myself for a long time. Broke in more than I can count."

"Nice. We had some growing up. Always well trained by the time we got them. Still, it's been a while." He glanced up at the barn. "Dylan used to have a pony and a donkey, I think."

He nodded, not sure what to say. Was the guy mentioning Dylan to try and warn him off or to see if he was interested in his friend? "She's enjoyed hanging out with Stormy and Blaze." He didn't mention how he'd enjoyed spending time with her too, how his every nerve lit up when she smiled, or how he couldn't stop thinking about the way she looked when she bit her lip in thought. Or about the fire in her voice when she talked about uncovering the truth. She burned too bright to ignore.

Nate nodded, brushing sand from his palms. "She's good like that. Always was. Dylan's the kind of person who steps in, whether it's wise or not."

That was obviously a warning. The words struck deeper than they should have. Not because they weren't true. But because Abe had started to believe that Dylan might be the first person in a long time who saw past his spotlight-induced shadow.

He studied Nate. The guy wasn't smug or possessive. He didn't seem like a man playing a game. Just... decent. Confident. The kind of guy who'd make your sister laugh or help your mother carry groceries. The kind of guy who wouldn't screw it up if Dylan gave him a chance. The kind of friend who would watch out for someone who'd been hurt before.

Which should've made this easier. But somehow, it made it worse.

He took a step closer. "She may seem tough on the outside, but with her history..." Nate's eyes met his. "I don't have to warn you to be careful with her. She's strong enough to watch out for herself, but I will say this. You hurt her, you'll no longer be welcome in this town."

Abe nodded slowly.

"Well," Nate said suddenly. He slipped his earbuds back in. "I'll let you get back to whatever you were doing. Just thought I'd say hi."

Abe nodded. "Take care."

He watched Nate jog away, shrinking quickly into the horizon where sky met surf.

A warning from the man was better than being told to back off because he was interested in Dylan. Wasn't it?

Abe turned and climbed the steps slowly, each one heavier than the last.

By the time he made it back to the house, the cold turkey sandwich waiting in the fridge seemed like a joke.

He grabbed a beer instead and sat down at the deck table, his eyes fixed on the gray ribbon of ocean beyond the dunes.

It wasn't Dylan's fault Nate made him feel like a second-string quarterback. He liked the guy even more after the warning not to hurt her. It showed that he cared. Cared in a non-sexual way. Like the brotherly way that Dylan had hinted at.

Dylan wasn't anyone's to claim.

Not yet.

Maybe not ever.

Nate was right that she could take care of herself.

But damn it... he wanted the job. Wanted to claim her as his own. There was that primordial desire flaring its evil head again.

Whatever happened now, he had two priorities: getting some answers about the night Kara died and making sure Dylan's name was kept out of the tabloids.

If anyone found out that he was getting closer to Dylan, who she was, what she did for a living, and why they had met, well, he didn't want to think about it. Not when his mind was filled with images of kissing her again and getting her into his bed.

He was trying to keep that from happening for a little longer. Really he was. At least until they had more answers. Until he knew that she had no doubt that he'd had nothing to do with Kara's death.

He was fairly sure that it was more for his benefit than hers. She held her suspicions close to her chest. Hell, he hadn't even had a clue why she was there until he'd seen her jogging that day on the beach and was positive that she had been the one who had run out of the house that night.

. . .

Half an hour later, he heard Dylan's car drive up the gravel driveway. To his happy surprise, she carried a few boxes from the local pizza place, Baked.

"You must have read my mind," he called out to her as she climbed the front steps. She glanced over and smiled at him as he rounded the building.

"I skipped lunch," she said, waving the boxes.

He met her at the door and opened it for her.

"You smell like the ocean and horses." She smiled when they stepped inside.

"I took a walk." He shrugged. "And spent time with Stormy and Blaze."

"Oh?" She set the boxes on the countertop. "How are they doing?"

"Great. I think I've finally got Blaze comfortable with a saddle."

"It was that easy?" She frowned.

"Easy?" He shook his head. "The bruises I got this last week are proof I worked for it." He laughed.

She opened the first box. "I hope you like meat lover's."

"Love it." He pulled out two plates. "Beer?"

She nodded and he walked over to the fridge as she plated a few slices of pizza.

"We can take this out on the back deck to watch the sunset," he suggested.

"Lead the way." She took the plates and followed him down the hallway.

"This is Max and Juliette's room?" she asked as they passed through.

"Yeah." He glanced over at her. "I'd give you a tour but..."

She chuckled. "Yeah, I've already been through here. Still, it was pretty dark." She stopped and looked at the painting of the lighthouse hanging over the bed. "Nice. Looks like one of Allison Jordan's pieces." She squinted and nodded. "Yup, very nice."

"There are a couple others throughout the place." He slid open the back glass door and waited until she stepped out.

As she sat down, he watched the sunlight slide over her hair and wished desperately to touch her again.

"You have questions?" he asked, settling into the chair across from her as he took a bite of pizza.

Dylan tucked her legs beneath her and angled towards him, eyes searching his face. The sunset bathed her in gold, softening the edges of her sharp focus, but he felt the shift in her. She wasn't here to flirt or make small talk. She was here for the truth.

"I do," she admitted after taking a sip of beer to wash down the bite of pizza. "Are you ready?"

He nodded, bracing himself as he took another sip of beer.

"What was Kara like, growing up? Who were her friends?" she asked.

He exhaled slowly, gaze drifting to the horizon. "She had a small circle. Reba was her best friend in college. She had a few others friends from before, but Kara wasn't the kind of person who needed a crowd. She was more... one-on-one. Quiet, but fierce once you knew her."

Dylan nodded slowly. "And her family?"

"Complicated," he said. "Her mom was strict, judgmental. Never approved of me or much else that Kara did. Her dad was passive. Sweet, but checked out. Kevin was... well, he was everything to her. Older. Protective to a fault. They'd argue sometimes, usually about me, or her life choices. But she loved him."

Dylan's expression tightened. "Did you and Kevin get along?"

Abe gave a short, humorless laugh. "At first, yes. It was one of the reasons I allowed him to stay with me for a few months. Then, after Kara and I started dating, not really. He didn't trust me after that. After I got the record deal, he thought that the spotlight I was about to enter would change our relationship. I think he already thought that I had changed her when we started dating."

"Had you?" she asked softly.

He glanced at her. "No. If anything, she changed me." He held back how much he'd been willing to give up for Kara. If she had asked him, he would have ripped up the contract and never recorded his first album.

A pause settled between them. The waves filled the silence for a moment before Dylan spoke again.

"That night... the night she died," she said carefully. "Tell me about it again."

"We went out that evening. We ate dinner at a local burger place, and we talked for a while about my music career. She was questioning if she should continue going to school. She had started nursing classes that fall to be an RN. It felt like... a reset for us. Like we'd finally stopped spinning in circles and had settled on what our future together would look like." He shifted slightly. "We did have a stupid argument about something." He shook his head, trying to remember. "I think it was my career. I wanted to hold off on going on tour until after..." He stopped and swallowed as he looked up at Dylan. "I wanted marriage. She didn't."

She nodded slightly. "Did you... make love that night?" Her voice was quieter now.

He shook his head slowly. "No. After dinner, she dropped me back off at my place. I'd had a couple beers and left my car at the restaurant." He set his fork down and met her eyes. "She said that she was tired and had class in the morning and didn't come in. Besides, my roommate was there. She kissed me and told me that she was proud of me for making a choice, for sticking it out. That's the last time I saw her."

Dylan studied him for a long moment, her eyes narrowing slightly. Her expression shifted, harder now, more clinical. Measured.

"The police report," she said carefully, "it said that there were signs that Kara had had sex shortly before her death."

Abe blinked and time stopped. He felt his heart sink into his gut.

Chapter Thirteen

Dylan watched Abe's face pale and knew instantly that he'd had no idea what the initial police report had claimed about Kara that night. Or that they had assumed that he had been the one to be intimate with her. This was another reason her family had looked at him closely. Her clothes had been torn from her and there were marks on her skin that didn't appear to have been caused by the accident.

Reaching out, she took his hand.

"Are you okay?"

He nodded and she watched him swallow a few times before standing up quickly and walking over to the railing on the deck. His hands gripped the railing like a vice, as if he could shatter the wood with his fingers.

She moved over to his side slowly, as if approaching a wounded animal.

"I... had a suspicion"—he sighed and glanced at her—"that she was seeing someone else. It's one of the reasons why we met that night. That and I was thinking about not going on tour. No one else knew, but..." He glanced sideways at her.

"You think she was seeing someone else?" She frowned and tried to process this new information.

His eyes met hers as he turned towards her fully and nodded once. "I noticed things. She would receive text messages and lie to me about who they were from. She would say she had to study for a test and when I asked how the test went, she forgot she had told me she had one." He closed his eyes and leaned on the railing a little more. "She was a terrible liar."

"Do you know who? Suspect anyone?" she asked, her heart jumping slightly. This could be the break they needed.

He shook his head and looked off as the sun sank lower over the horizon. "No, no idea. Maybe Kevin would know." He took a deep breath as she watched him carefully.

Kevin. The man was pissing her off. Not only had he flaked at their meeting in Edgeview, the one that he had requested, but the next morning he'd called and made an excuse about going to a bar and losing his phone.

There was no doubt in her mind now that Abe had nothing to do with Kara's death. She'd wanted to believe that the moment she'd been hired, but now she knew it down to her very core.

"You said she would get text messages?" she asked. When he nodded, she moved back over to her bag and pulled out her computer. "If you knew it, would you recognize someone's number if you saw it?"

He moved over and sat down next to her as she flipped open her computer screen and pulled up the official report, scanning ahead for the phone logs.

"Here." She motioned with her finger. "These numbers

I was unable to track down. They're from a burner number and are no longer in use."

He frowned. "I know a few industry people use burner numbers but those don't look familiar, and, well..." He glanced at her. "Don't drug dealers use those too?"

She smiled and nodded. "Yes, but mainly in TV shows and movies. Still, they can be used by anyone. I tracked the number to a phone that was purchased at a gas station in Lakeview just outside of LA."

"My old townhouse was in that area. Kara's place was closer to the college."

"Yeah, which is why the police thought..." She dropped off.

"That I had purchased the phone," he jumped in quickly. "Right."

"The text messages were somewhat cryptic. Meeting times, places, but..." She clicked the keyboard. "This last one pretty much cleared your name." She showed him.

"Just dropped him off."

"We need to talk. I can't do this much longer. Everyone is getting suspicious." Kara replied.

"I'll head to our usual spot."

"Fine, but I'm tired of pretending with him." Kara had responded.

"Just a little longer, then I'll leave her for good and we can be together like we want," came the response.

She felt her stomach swirl at the low sound emanating from Abe's chest. Was it pain or anger? Hard to tell.

"What does that mean?" He glanced over at her. "I'm tired of pretending with him?" He didn't give her a chance to answer. Instead, he added, "Who is he going to leave? A wife?"

She nodded slowly. "I also assumed from some of the

other messages that whoever Kara was seeing was married or at least in a long-term relationship."

"Why was she with me? We weren't married or engaged. Why didn't he want her to leave me?"

"My guess is they wanted to wait until after you'd hit it big." She knew it stung, so she was surprised when Abe didn't flinch or act hurt.

"Why did it matter? She had nothing to do with my career."

She shrugged. "I was hoping you shed some light on that area. Was anything going on in Kara's life at that time?"

"She had just started fall classes." He glanced out to the water. "I was the one who had a lot going on at that point. I'd just finished my first record a few months back. Tony had a bunch of PR stunts lined up for me once we were done. They had released my first single a few months earlier and it was climbing the charts. So they were very hopeful for the full album."

She smiled. "And it hit number one quicker than any other new artist in the past decade."

His eyebrows shot up. "So you had heard of me before?"

She chuckled. "Okay, full confession time. I've loved your music from day one."

His smile spread slowly and he shifted towards her. "I would have never pegged you as a fan. I can usually spot one from a mile away."

She rolled her eyes. "Anyone who has heard you sing is a fan. Then you add all this"—she waved her hand over him—"prettiness and sexy natural swagger you have and boom!" She snapped her fingers. "I along with every other red-blooded woman was an insta-fan."

He shifted even closer, his grin spreading, and her insides fluttered. "You acted pretty cool at first."

She rolled her eyes. "I'm very practiced. But honestly, it drove me nuts. You drive me nuts."

He tilted his head as if thinking for a moment. "How nuts?"

She glanced at his lips. "About as crazy as when you kissed me."

His smile slipped a little. "You were the one driving me crazy at that point." His hand came up to cup her face. "Still are." His eyes moved to her lips. "My heart skips each time I think of kissing you." He reached for her hand and placed her palm on his chest. "Feel what you're doing to me now."

She did. His heartbeat matched her own erratic one as he leaned in and brushed his lips across hers.

"How many more questions do you have for me tonight?" he asked, resting his forehead against hers.

"None," she answered quickly.

"There are some things I can see clearly written in your eyes." He leaned back, searching her eyes.

"Such as?"

"You no longer think I had anything to do with Kara's last night." He brushed a strand of her hair aside.

"I..." She started to tell him she'd never believed he had anything to do with Kara's death, but instead just shook her head. "Does that matter to you?"

"It's the most important thing in my world," he said before kissing her again.

She melted and purred with desire. How did he have so much control over her? Why did her body have to respond this way when it never had before? Why him?

Her mind switched gears as his tongue played over hers. She no longer needed proof or evidence that Abe had nothing to hide. She knew she had more secrets in her closet than he did.

When he pressed his hard body up against hers, her mind stopped working as her needs outweighed every thought. More, was all she could think. I need to feel more.

She couldn't remember the last time she'd felt so... much.

Abe's hands roamed over her, gently tugging her shirt up until his fingertips brushed against her skin. She moaned with delight.

His mouth trailed down her neck. "Dylan, I didn't come here tonight for this."

"A bonus then," she said, sliding her fingers into his hair to keep him tight against her.

He chuckled at her move and then stilled when she reached down and covered him, trailing her fingers gently over his length. He was hard, pressing against his jeans, and she felt her insides quiver at the thought of feeling him inside her.

She jerked free and stood up, then took his hand. "Abe, take me to bed."

He wrapped his arms around her and held on for a moment before leading her back into the house and into the bedroom he was staying in.

There, he pulled her back into his arms and kissed her until her knees went weak. Then he lifted her into his arms and gently laid her on the bed.

He surprised her by slowly removing her shoes and then taking his time to run his hands over her legs.

He glanced up at her. "Sexiest legs in the world." He smiled up at her.

"You're a leg man?" she said as his hands moved up to her thighs.

"Not really, but wow, I can't ignore sexy when I see it." His fingertips skimmed her inner thighs.

She closed her eyes and leaned back while he snaked his fingertips under her shorts.

"Abe," she moaned when he tugged her shorts down and continued to explore her with his hands and lips.

He spread his hand on her stomach and gently nudged her back until she was lying on his bed.

When he tugged her panties aside and used his mouth on her, she arched and cried out as she wrapped her legs around his shoulders.

Too much. So many thoughts and feelings flooded her mind. Then his tongue rolled over her clit and everything shut down. Thoughts. Feelings. Questions. Everything exploded until there was only him.

While she tried to catch her breath, Abe shifted over her on the bed, pulling her farther up as he covered her completely.

She tugged his shirt off, her nails scraping his skin as her demands grew.

"I need you, now," she said, locking her legs around his hips as she trailed kisses down his collarbone.

When he shifted and slid into her, she felt at home for the first time in her life. This, this was where she belonged. Where she fit. Where she wanted to be for the rest of her life.

Then a moment later, her world exploded again, and she knew that nothing else in the world mattered. Only Abe.

That thought scared the shit out of her. After her body cooled, Abe shifted to her side and held her close.

"I can tell that you're already rethinking this," Abe said into her hair.

"No." She instantly denied it. "No," she said a little softer, trying to relax her body. "I'm just scared of what it, what you, make me feel."

He was silent for a moment. "What do I make you feel?"

She closed her eyes and took a deep breath before answering. "Safe."

He shifted until he was looking down at her.

"You didn't feel safe?"

She shrugged. "I'm not scared." She felt the need to explain. "Just..." God, why was this so hard? "Wandering."

His eyes narrowed slightly. "Like you don't belong anywhere?"

She nodded slowly. "Being back in town, sleeping in my old bed, it's... empty almost. Without him there, it's just an old building where the plumbing shakes the walls when I use the dishwasher and washing machine, and the floorboards creak. Every single floorboard." She rolled her eyes.

He smiled down at her, and she lifted her hands to run her fingers through his hair again. Then she brought him down and kissed him, holding her lips to his. "But this, this feels like home. Oddly."

He tilted his head and seemed to be thinking about it for a moment. "Scares the shit out of me, personally."

She smiled. "Ditto." She rested her head back as he ran his eyes over her slowly.

"I have a thing I'm supposed to go to this weekend. It's just one night. LA. Lights, drama, free food." His eyebrows rose slightly. "It might be possible to get some answers from a few people in the circles Kara and I were in back in the day."

Her eyebrows rose. "Are you asking me to go to LA with you, on a date?"

He smiled. "Yeah, if you want. Plus," he jumped in quickly, "like I said, a few people who were close to Kara will be there. Maybe even the man she was with."

"Count me in," she answered quickly.

Chapter Fourteen

Holding Dylan as she slept was one of the best feelings in the world. Her words played over in his head as he drifted off, making him dream of danger and darkness, only to be saved by the sight of her.

When the sun started streaming in the window, she had already abandoned the bed, and he could hear the water running in his bathroom.

He was trying to figure out how to keep her there for the day, but when she came out of the bathroom, she was fully dressed.

When she noticed he was awake, she stilled. He could see that she felt uncomfortable.

"I... need to head to Portland for a few days. If I'm going to go with you on Friday, I have some... details to tie up."

He stood up and walked over to her, then wrapped his arms around her and kissed her until he felt her body melt against his. God, he could get addicted to this feeling, the way she gave in, the way she fit against him like they'd been designed for one other.

"Go. Do what you have to. I'll be here," he murmured,

pressing a final kiss to her temple. "Our flight leaves Friday at ten in the morning."

She nodded, brushing her fingers along his jaw. "I'll be back Thursday night," she promised, then she stepped away, slowly, like it physically hurt her to leave.

He pulled on his clothes and walked her to the door. Watching her drive away left him hollow in a way he hadn't expected. Even after just one night with her, one perfect, tangled, laugh-filled night, it felt like something permanent had settled into his bones.

He stood at the door for a few minutes after the sound of her car faded down the road, staring out at the slow sway of the trees along the cliffs.

Then he got to work.

Tending to the horses grounded him. Blaze gave him attitude for showing up late for feed time, and Misty nuzzled at his pockets with practiced pickpocket finesse.

He took both out for exercise until they were all sweaty and worn out. By the time he finished cooling them off and refilling water troughs and spreading new straw, his muscles were warm and his mind had quieted.

Next, he tackled the yard around the lighthouse, a sprawling, stubborn patch of land that Max had clearly overestimated when he bought the damn mower. The machine looked more like a spaceship than a piece of lawn equipment. It had a touch screen, GPS mapping, and a warning label in six languages.

It also made Abe curse like a sailor for the first fifteen minutes.

Once he got the hang of it, though, there was something peaceful about the work. He was now thinking of getting the same mower for his place.

He loved the smell of fresh-cut grass, the distant cry of

Art of Love

gulls, the hum of the ocean meeting the shore below. He took his time, edging the old pathways near the lighthouse and clearing the overgrown slope by the west cliff. By late afternoon, he was sunburned, sore, and satisfied.

Thursday morning, with the chores mostly caught up, he headed into town for milk, coffee, and maybe something frozen that wasn't cold turkey sandwiches.

In a small town where people tended to know everyone's business, he still managed to get second glances. He should have worn a ball cap and sunglasses.

It started with a couple in the parking lot, older, visiting from out of town, judging by the matching T-shirts that read Pride: A Whale of a Good Time! The woman nudged the man, whispered, then turned towards him with wide eyes.

Abe ducked his head and moved faster, slipping into the grocery store like he was avoiding the paparazzi.

He wasn't in the mood for selfies. Not today.

This morning he'd made a list of potential men Kara could have been seeing. Besides himself.

The emotional bomb that Dylan had dropped on him the other night about Kara sleeping with someone the night that she'd died had him rethinking their entire time together.

Now his mind kept replaying that news on a loop while his body shuffled through Pride's local grocery store like a grumpy incognito celebrity. Since he didn't have a hat, he pulled his hoodie up to hide some of his face.

He was halfway through the produce aisle when he heard it, the unmistakable sound of two people failing very badly at whispering.

"Oh my god. That's him."

"From the underwear ads?"

"And the music video where he's playing guitar shirtless in the rain!"

He groaned. He hated that video, but it had made him who he was today. A star.

"Ugh, why does he have to look that good buying lettuce?"

Abe set the lettuce down and hunched deeper into his hoodie like it was a cloak of invisibility. It was not.

He quickly snatched a pre-made Caesar salad container, pivoted fast, and made a break for the frozen food aisle. Two teen girls tracked him down there like heat-seeking missiles, phones out, giggling.

One of them called out, "Hey, Abe! Drop the hoodie. We saw everything in those ads anyway!"

He groaned, veered left, and took a hard detour into an aisle that sold air fresheners and novelty items. A cardboard cutout of a smiling cowboy pushing barbecue sauce startled him, and for a second he thought it might ask for a selfie too.

He finally reached the checkout line, where a toddler in the cart ahead of him pointed at Abe's hoodie and shouted, "Mommy, that's him!" The kid then pointed to a tabloid magazine that showed his face and the words "Abe's Secret Love Affairs" under it.

The mother's eyes widened and then her face blushed bright red.

When the teens rounded the corner, she stiffened and frowned.

"Go ahead of me. I'll fend them off for you," she whispered. She blocked the teens from knocking him over.

"Taylor, Leslie, don't you have classes today?" the mother asked in a stern tone.

The teens looked torn, but after the clerk started scanning his items, they turned and walked out of the building.

"Thanks," he said, and handed the kid a sucker from the checkout area. "On me," he told the clerk, and winked at the mother.

After paying for his purchases, he grabbed his change, mumbled "thank you," and bolted to his truck like his jeans were on fire.

Once safely inside, he texted Dylan:

Miss you. Also, remind me never to go anywhere without a fake beard and dark glasses.

He tossed the phone aside and drove home, watching the quaint little town of Pride shrink in his rearview mirror. Fame had its perks. Grocery shopping wasn't one of them.

Later, the house was quiet except for the soft hum of the record player in the living room spinning something bluesy and tragic. Abe was sunk into the couch, beer in hand, barefoot, and still emotionally tangled up from the past few days.

His mind played over that last night with Kara like it had often over the years. But this time he thought about it with all the new knowledge.

They'd gone out to that little burger place just outside of town, the one she liked. The one with the paper tablecloths and crayons at every table. She'd drawn a guitar and had written "Soon, you'll be famous and forget me" in loopy cursive beneath it.

At the time, he'd thought she meant he would leave her behind once his music career grew and he was famous. He'd taken it as a sign that she believed in him, that she was proud of him and willing to make sacrifices for his future. He had promised her that he would never leave her, which had her frowning and looking down at their joined hands.

But now... now he wondered if she'd been trying to

soften the blow. Letting him down gently before she disappeared for good.

Maybe what she really meant was: You'll get over me, after I break your heart.

He remembered how tense he'd been later that night. He'd asked her straight up, "Are you seeing someone else?" He'd heard her talking on the phone, had seen a few text messages that she'd kept from him. With all the lies she'd told him about where she'd been and with whom, he'd known something was off.

She'd laughed, not meanly, just sort of surprised. "Of course not," she'd assured him.

But she'd paused half a second too long. Just enough for doubt to slip in.

She'd reached across the table, touched his hand. "I want you to finish this album. You're so close to making it big. You've worked so hard on recording all the songs. You have to see this through."

He'd mistaken that for support. Now it felt like a distraction. Like she was waving one hand while the other was reaching for the doorknob.

She had driven him back to his place after dinner, because he'd had a few beers. The second one had been to work up the courage to confront her about cheating on him.

He could still feel the press of her lips on his under the dim orange parking lot lights. Her hands in his hair, the heat of her body close but not close enough.

It was funny that now, as he thought of those times, he realized they paled in comparison to the night he'd had with Dylan. They fell short of the heat Dylan made him feel by just being in the same room as him.

He'd been young and dumb. He'd wanted to fall in love. Needed it. Now he knew better. If he was going to fall in love, it wasn't because he was desperate. It was going to be for real this time.

Kara had pulled back first. "I should go. It's late, and I have class in the morning."

He'd let her go and stood in the freshly rained-on parking lot as her headlights faded down the street.

She had always texted him when she got home.

Made it. Love you.

That was the ritual.

But that night... nothing.

He'd waited, phone in hand, drowsy but stubborn. Eventually, the exhaustion won. He fell asleep without ever getting her message. Or realizing it would never come.

Now he knew she'd had sex with someone else that night. The man she'd been seeing. Had their relationship been full of lies? How long had she been cheating? Had she just been using him? Why?

And who the hell had she been with?

Had she been planning to leave him all along? Had she ever loved him?

His gut twisted. The things she'd said, the things he'd thought were encouragement, maybe they were just polite lies. Maybe she'd already made her choice and was just waiting for the right moment to vanish.

Abe stood and walked to the window, staring out at the dark curve of the cliffs in the distance. The night seemed heavier than usual, as if even the stars were keeping secrets.

He didn't want to hate her. God, he didn't. But love, twisted by betrayal, left a scar that burned every time he tried to remember Kara without bitterness.

And now that scar was flaring hot.

Who had she gone to that night?

And why had she lied?

He was so lost in thought that at first he didn't notice the lights heading towards the house. Then came the familiar crunch of gravel as Dylan's car parked next to his.

He walked over and opened the door just as Dylan stepped up to it. She looked wind-tossed and road-weary, but she still managed a tired smile that sent something warm and painful straight to his chest.

"Hi," he said, pulling her into a hug before she could even set her bag down.

"Hi. I almost hit a deer on the way down from Portland, but I managed to save Bambi's mother just in time." She smiled.

He kissed the side of her head. "Want a drink? Or just to collapse?"

"Collapse," she muttered, then pulled back, more serious now. "But first... I found something."

She crossed to the sofa, pulled out her phone, and scrolled through her notes.

"I got confirmation of what Kevin did after Kara died." She glanced over at him. "He didn't just disappear. He checked himself into a rehab center the week after the funeral."

Abe blinked. "That's why he stopped pursuing me as Kara's killer? Why I stopped hearing from him after her death?"

"Exactly. He'd been spiraling for a while, apparently. His parents covered for him and did a damn good job too. Not only were they dealing with the death of their daughter, they were trying to reset their only son. It also explains why he suddenly stopped pushing for the police to go after you. He was in a treatment center, off the grid."

Abe sat down next to her slowly, his mind whirling at the new information. "That explains part of it. But... what if he was involved that night somehow? What if Kevin was the one driving? What if he'd been drinking?" As soon as he said it, he dismissed it. Kara hadn't allowed him to drive that night because of the two beers. He doubted she'd let her brother drive her drunk. Also, there was the little matter of who she'd have sex with.

Dylan shook her head. "That crossed my mind too. In the original police report, Kevin said he was home alone the entire night. Plus, that doesn't explain who Kara was with... before the accident." Her eyes locked on his and he shifted slightly.

"Yeah, I guess it doesn't make sense. Kevin being at home was never confirmed, was it? Did they just take his word for it because they were busy pointing fingers at me?"

Dylan exhaled and looked up at him. "Never officially confirmed, no. It's thin, his alibi. His parents could've covered for him too. He had motive—resentment, Kara always defending you—and he was drinking."

Abe rubbed the back of his neck. "Hell... we've all been looking at this through the wrong lens. Maybe Kevin wasn't just grieving? Maybe he was guilt driven?"

They sat there in thick silence for a moment, the old record softly crackling in the background.

Finally, Dylan looked over. "When we get back... I plan to stay in Portland for another night. I have scheduled a meeting with Kevin. Apparently, he is back in the city."

Abe gave a slow nod. "Good. Can I listen in?"

She nodded slowly. "I'll clear it with him first."

"Thanks."

He was done letting questions go unanswered. He wasn't going to let anyone hide the truth any longer. No matter the cost.

Chapter Fifteen

"This is a private jet." Dylan gasped, adjusting the straps of her well-worn backpack, which held an extra pair of jeans, a T-shirt, sleeping shorts and shirt, and her small makeup bag. She stood staring up at the sleek white plane gleaming under the morning sun, in shock.

"Yeah," Abe said casually, as if he hadn't just blown her mind. He slipped his hand into hers, warm and steady. "I thought I told you."

"You said we were flying," she whispered. "You didn't say we were being wined and dined like celebrities." She blinked up at the luxury aircraft again. "You left that part out."

He grinned, clearly enjoying her reaction. "Don't hold it against me."

"Never," she whispered as they climbed the stairs.

The interior of the jet was ridiculously plush, with cream leather seats, wood paneling that probably cost more than her car, and a flight attendant who offered them mimosas the second they stepped onboard. Dylan barely had time to sink into her seat before they were airborne, cruising smoothly above the clouds while the attendant brought them warm croissants and fresh fruit like they were royalty.

"Is this your usual travel situation?" she asked, eyeing him over the rim of her mimosa.

Abe smirked. "Only when PR's paying the bill."

"Remind me to thank your publicist later," she muttered.

Abe chuckled and lifted his glass in a mock toast. "Tony will appreciate that. Especially if you say it in public where he can claim full credit."

Once the jet leveled out at their cruising altitude, a flight attendant brought over a spread that looked like it belonged in a five-star restaurant rather than 35,000 feet in the air. Freshly scrambled eggs, crisp bacon, tiny stacks of pancakes with real maple syrup, and flaky pastries that made Dylan almost forget she was nervous.

"Okay," she said, biting into a croissant that nearly melted in her mouth. "This is officially the best breakfast I've ever had."

"Better than the scones at Sara's Nook that you're so fond of?" he teased, reaching for a slice of melon.

She snorted. "Unless Sara recently started using truffle butter, yeah this wins."

They ate leisurely, the sky stretched out around them in a soft blue haze. With nowhere to rush off to, and no crowds pressing in, the atmosphere felt almost... intimate.

"So," she asked between sips of orange juice, "your ranch. Is that where you keep your herd of fans?"

He laughed. "Nope. Just my horses, a dog named Ringo who thinks he's in charge, and a neighbor who thinks I'm secretly a vampire."

"That tracks." She chuckled.

He leaned back, stretching his long legs out in front of him. "The ranch is in Santa Ynez. I bought it a few years ago after I wrapped up my second tour. I needed space to breathe. And hay, apparently."

She smiled, watching him soften as he spoke. "Sounds peaceful."

"It is. Mornings there are quiet. I can go a whole day without hearing anything but birds and Carson whining at the fence because he wants carrots. I am getting spoiled by the smell of the ocean at Max and Juliette's place though."

"You named your horse Carson?" she grinned.

"Don't judge. I was going through a phase. I have a few more horses with normal names, like Leo and Carl."

She laughed and shook her head. "Did you buy the place before or after the underwear ads?"

He shot her a look, amused and mildly horrified. "Don't bring that up while I'm eating."

"I mean, it's a valid career milestone. You're like a triple threat now. Music, modeling, and... ranching?"

He gave a self-deprecating shrug. "I'm just trying to keep all the parts of my life from burning down at the same time."

She watched him for a moment, this man who the world saw as polished and untouchable, who somehow still managed to be grounded. Real. Hers, for now.

"You're doing okay," she said softly.

He glanced at her, something flickering behind his eyes. Gratitude, maybe. Or something deeper.

The rest of the flight passed in warm conversation, laughter, and the quiet hum of something unspoken between them. Something that felt dangerously close to falling.

And Dylan, somewhere between coffee refills and cloud watching, realized she didn't mind the fall at all.

When they landed in LA, a sleek black limo was already waiting for them at the private terminal. Dylan's sneakers squeaked on the polished pavement as she climbed in, tugging self-consciously at her hoodie. She felt like a fraud, just a small-town girl who didn't own a single silk dress or diamond. But Abe looked completely at ease, sunglasses on, arm slung around her shoulders like he belonged to this sleek world. And maybe, when he looked at her like that, she did too.

The hotel was downtown and looked like a palace. The lobby ceiling soared like a cathedral's, with chandeliers big enough to need their own zip code. Staff greeted Abe by name and handed her a glass of champagne before she could even open her mouth.

They were shown into a private elevator by a bellboy who carried their luggage on one of those rolling carts. Even though it was just her small bag and Abe's duffle bag, the man treated them like they were fragile vases.

Then he opened the door to the suite.

"Oh my god," she whispered, stepping into the marble-floored entrance. The space was bigger than her entire apartment in Portland, not to mention the cabin home she'd grown up in and was currently occupying in Pride. She stepped into the sunken living room, which had floor-to-ceiling windows with a view of the city skyline. Next to it was a dining table set for ten, and a balcony with a hot tub. There were two bedrooms that sat across from one another, each with their own bathrooms, which were the fanciest things she'd ever seen.

"Oh my god," she said again, this time pointing at the

rack of dresses waiting in the corner like couture soldiers at attention. "What are those for?"

"You." Abe took her hands in his.

"What is happening?" she whispered.

"They sent along some options in your size for the party tonight, along with a stylist, who should be here soon," Abe said, smiling.

"Is this real?" she whispered, feeling a little like Cinderella waiting for her fairy godmother to wave her wand.

Before he could answer, there was a knock on the door. He opened it and in came a team of hair and makeup professionals and a stylist who greeted her like they were old friends. Abe was ushered out before she could protest.

"I'll see you soon," he said, giving her a quick kiss as he slipped out, somehow managing to make jeans and a plain T-shirt look like a fashion statement.

She was pushed down into a plush velvet chair before she could even process what was happening. Her backpack was long forgotten in the corner of the massive suite. Two stylists immediately flanked her like a pit crew at a race. One tugged gently at her hair with deft fingers, murmuring about texture and shine, while the other surveyed her face like it was a blank canvas about to be turned into a piece of art.

Someone refilled her champagne glass before she'd even made it halfway through the first. The bubbles tickled her nose as she sipped, trying not to fidget for the stylists.

The hairstylist curled her hair into soft, romantic waves, each lock coaxed into shape with a gentle tug and a spritz of something that smelled expensive and a little like jasmine. The makeup brushes swept across her cheeks, her lids, and her lips, so soft and precise she nearly melted into the chair.

If they hadn't been chatting softly about contouring and red carpet lighting, she might have dozed off entirely.

By the time they were done, she hardly recognized herself. Her skin glowed, her eyes looked impossibly wide and bright, and her lips, glossed with something called "Starlit Rose" looked kissable in a way that made her blush to notice.

Then came the rack of dresses.

The dresses had been picked through by the stylist at one point and narrowed down to a couple choices while she'd been under the spell of soft bristles and styling wands. Every color shimmered under the crystal lights. Sequins, silk, lace, and chiffon all draped like promises waiting to be broken.

She looked over the half dozen options, trailing a finger over the expensive fabrics like she didn't belong in the room. But when she spotted the midnight blue cocktail dress, she stopped cold.

Plunging neckline. Open back. Delicate beadwork traced the hem like constellations. It was elegant but bold, sleek but with just enough sparkle to make her feel like a walking secret.

She hesitated for only a second then pulled it from the rack and slipped into the next room to put it on.

When she emerged a few minutes later, she actually forgot to breathe.

The dress hugged her body like it had been custom-made for her. The hem skimmed the middle of her thighs, revealing legs she'd never thought much about before but which suddenly felt like an asset. The legs that Abe had fixated on and enjoyed so much.

The fabric of the dress clung to her waist, dipped low

across her back, and plunged just daringly enough in the front to make her heat.

She turned slowly in front of the mirror, her heart thudding.

She looked... stunning. Not like herself. Or maybe exactly like the version of herself she'd always hoped to become.

She was still adjusting the thin strap on her shoulder when the suite door clicked open behind her.

Abe walked in, half-distracted as he shrugged into his jacket. He froze mid-step when he saw her. Damn, her mouth watered instantly at the sight of him in a black suit with a blue tie that seemed to match her dress perfectly.

His mouth parted slightly. "Holy..." He blinked, cleared his throat. "You look..."

She waited, her heart thudding hard. "Like I stole this dress?"

"Like I'm going to have to fight off half the room tonight," he said, his voice low, reverent.

A slow smile spread across her lips, her nerves replaced by a flicker of heat. "You clean up nicely yourself."

He did. The black tailored suit fit him perfectly. He looked like he belonged on the red carpet. But it was the way he looked at her like the rest of the world had fallen away that made her feel completely out of place and exactly where she belonged, all at once.

She smoothed her hands over the dress, her fingers trembling just slightly. "I've never had anything like this happen before."

He stepped closer, brushing a curl from her cheek. "Get used to it."

Just then, there was another knock on the door. Abe turned, already halfway to the door, and cracked it open.

"Ah, perfect timing," he said.

Dylan tilted her head, curious, as four people stepped into the suite, all dressed in sleek black attire and each carrying what looked like armored briefcases. They moved with the precision and quiet grace of professionals used to high stakes and higher expectations.

They set the heavy cases on the glass coffee table in the sitting area with practiced care, then flipped them open with a soft click-click.

Dylan gasped.

Inside, nestled in black velvet, were rows upon rows of glittering diamonds, polished gold, and gemstones in colors she'd only ever seen behind security glass or on the necks of people accepting awards on TV. Earrings sparkled like stars. Bracelets coiled like delicate golden vines. There was a sapphire choker so vivid it looked like it had been carved out of the Pacific.

She took a step forward, stunned. "Is this...?"

"A loan from Cartier," one of the women explained with a professional smile. "Compliments of Mr. Carson's team. We were told to match the dress options."

Dylan stared at the display. "I own socks that don't match. This is next-level."

Abe chuckled from across the room, clearly enjoying her reaction.

"Would you like some help selecting a set?" the woman asked.

"Um, yes?" Dylan said, still not quite believing this was her life.

With gentle precision, the stylist selected a pair of teardrop diamond earrings and a delicate bracelet that looked like it was spun from moonlight. Then she added a platinum ring with a pear-shaped sapphire that mirrored the midnight hue of Dylan's dress and fastened a matching necklace around her neck. The cool weight of the jewels settled onto her skin like a crown.

She turned slowly to face the mirror again.

Her breath caught.

Between the shimmering curls, the plunging neckline, and now the diamonds glittering against her collarbone she looked like someone out of a movie. No, a fairytale.

And still, despite all the luxury and sparkle, it was the way that Abe was looking at her, like nothing in those cases could outshine her natural self, that made her feel truly priceless.

"I'm afraid to move," she whispered.

Abe stepped behind her, his hands settling lightly on her waist. "Then don't. Just stay like this."

She laughed, her voice a little breathless. "How is this real?"

"I'm asking myself the same thing," he murmured and then spun her around and kissed her.

For a single suspended moment, it didn't matter where they were going or who was watching. She wasn't just Dylan the detective, the one used to chasing leads, watching shitty hotel rooms, or digging through case files. She was a woman standing in a dress that fit like a dream, dripping in millions of dollars' worth of borrowed diamonds, with a man who looked at her like she was the only song he'd ever want to write.

And for tonight, that was enough.

"Dylan..."

His voice was low, reverent, and the way his gaze moved over her sent a rush of warmth straight through her.

She cleared her throat and smoothed her hands down

the satin fabric. "I feel like a movie extra who wandered into the wrong scene."

He shook his head. "You look like the lead actress, the one no one will be able to take their eyes off."

Her stomach fluttered, and suddenly the glittering suite, the dress, the champagne, it all faded to background noise. All she could see was him.

She still felt out of place, but when Abe looked at her like that, like she was the only thing in the world that mattered?

She knew that she didn't want to be anywhere else.

Chapter Sixteen

The moment they stepped into the party, Abe wished they could turn around and leave. Of course, there were plenty of camera flashes outside. His name was shouted and question after question was thrown his way.

"Who's the mystery woman, Abe?"

"Is that your new girlfriend?"

"Will you be performing tonight?"

"Are the rumors true about another tour?"

"When does your next album come out?"

He kept one hand lightly on the small of Dylan's back, steering her with a practiced smile and a quiet "just keep walking" under his breath. She didn't flinch or fumble, just kept her chin lifted like she belonged, like the million-dollar necklace around her neck was no big deal. God, she was handling this better than he was.

Once inside, the noise shifted. Softer, richer. Classier, but still overwhelming.

Hollywood and music legends filled the space like it was a red carpet come to life. The room was all marble floors, gold accents, and too many chandeliers for a single ceiling. A grand piano stood near one wall next to a string quartet that had clearly been hired more for ambiance than entertainment. Waitstaff floated through the room like black-clad ghosts, balancing trays of champagne flutes, smoked salmon canapés, and artfully sculpted desserts that looked too pretty to eat.

Abe hated all of it.

He'd been here before more times than he wanted to count and it always felt the same. Plastic smiles. Hollow congratulations. Men in thousand-dollar suits trying to talk music like they actually listened to the lyrics. Women clinging to his arm like he was still that guy from the underwear ad.

But tonight was different.

Tonight, Dylan was here.

She turned her head, catching his gaze over her shoulder as a jazz version of a pop hit floated through the air. Her eyes were wide but not scared. Curious. Lit up. And suddenly, it didn't feel quite so suffocating.

They made it halfway across the room when a familiar producer, the host of the party tonight, cut him off with a smile too wide to be real. "Abe Collins in the flesh. I was starting to think you were going to stay a recluse."

"Maybe I should have," Abe muttered, shaking the man's hand while his other arm stayed locked around Dylan's waist.

"Glad you made it. Hey, if the mood strikes, give us a song tonight?"

Abe opened his mouth to brush it off, but then caught Dylan's eyes again—bright, amused, encouraging. Damn it.

"We'll see," he said.

By the time dessert rolled around—tiny chocolate pyramids with gold leaf and something that tasted vaguely like passionfruit—the piano had been cleared of its string quartet and a mic had been set up. It was funny, no other hit singer in the place had been asked by the host to sing tonight. Was this a good sign?

"Looks like you're on the spot," Dylan whispered, brushing her hand against his.

Their host was motioning him to the stage area. He sighed and ran a hand through his hair before promising, "I'll make it quick."

He walked up and took the mic, and the room gradually quieted around him like a held breath. He was handed a guitar and adjusted the mic, letting his fingers hover over the strings. A thousand memories flooded his chest of his nights on tour, quiet bar gigs, music written in grief and healing, but none of them felt like this moment.

He didn't introduce the song. Didn't need to.

"This is a new one," he said and then he began to play.

It was him, the guitar, his voice, and the words he'd written with Dylan on his mind.

The chords were simple but honest. The melody soft and aching. And when he started singing, his voice was raw with feelings, in the best way.

No one had heard the song yet.

He was just a man talking about the moment he started breathing again, when the shadows began to lift and something warm stepped into his life. A laugh he didn't know he needed. A woman who didn't flinch from his worst, who called him out and still stayed. Who saw him when he barely saw himself.

He didn't look at the crowd as he sang. He looked at her.

She stood in the middle of the room, lips parted, chest rising slowly. Like she knew.

When the last note faded, there was a beat of silence, then an eruption of applause. A few cheers. Someone tried to get a video, but security stepped in.

Abe stood, gave a small nod, and returned to her side without a word.

"You wrote that for me," Dylan said softly, her voice barely above the hum of chatter.

He reached for her hand. "I didn't plan to."

She looked up at him, eyes shining. "Abe Collins, you're full of surprises."

He leaned close to her ear, his breath warm against her skin. "Stick around. I've got a few more happy surprises left in me."

And for the first time that night, he didn't want to leave the party. He wanted to stay exactly where he was, with her. Champagne, chandeliers, fake smiles and all. Because as long as she was there, everything felt real.

"There he is." James walked towards him, Reba following a few feet behind. James slapped him on the shoulder and then gave him one of those stupid hugs men gave each other when they don't really mean it.

It was funny, before the accident, Kara and Abe had been best friends with James and Reba. Later, after Abe had boosted James' career, the man had become more distant. The couple pulled away further after Kara's death. He'd believed at first that it was because they thought that he had something to do with Kara's death. After his career really took off, he no longer cared as long as James kept things professional.

"This must be Dylan...?" James said when he straightened and extended a hand towards her.

"Beck, Dylan Beck," she answered, shaking his hand.

"Right." James's eyes narrowed but then Reba stepped up. "James Lyle, and this is my wife, Reba."

"Kara and I were best friends," Reba said in a tone that was a little too sharp. Abe saw James wince slightly and take his wife's arm. It was obvious that Reba was already more than a few drinks in.

Dylan didn't miss a beat and just smiled as if she hadn't heard what Reba had said.

"On that note, I think I'm going to take her home." James wrapped his arm around his wife.

Before they could turn to go, however, Tony walked over. "You aren't leaving yet," he told James and Reba.

"Yeah, I'm going to get her home." James motioned towards Reba, who had grabbed two more drinks from a tray.

"Bummer." Tony glanced at him and Dylan. "Oh, this must be the new arm candy," Tony said with a wink.

Abe could have punched him.

James used the distraction to steer his wife towards the door after handing off the two still full glasses to a waiter.

"That new bit, you didn't mention you had that in your arsenal," Tony said. He noticed that Tony didn't bother to introduce himself to Dylan. No doubt because the man believed she wouldn't stick around for long.

"It's not for sale." He quickly wrapped his arm around Dylan's waist and pulled her closer. "A one-time performance."

"Too bad. You had the crowd wanting more." Tony took a glass of champagne and handed it to Dylan. "Pretty ladies should always have a drink in their hands." He winked at her.

Abe smiled when Dylan immediately set it down. "I've had my fill tonight. Thanks."

Before Tony could reply, someone across the room called him and he disappeared in the crowd.

"I should have warned you about him," Abe said softly.

Dylan chuckled. "I spotted him a mile away." She shrugged. "Now, how about we have a dance? Then you can introduce me to the most famous person here that you know." She purred as she wrapped her arms around his shoulders and brushed her body against his.

Every thought he had about staying at the party disappeared.

"I have a better idea." He ran his hands up to her waist. "What do you say we head back to our room, and I see what sexy things you are wearing under that dress?"

She smiled and then brushed her lips across his.

"I'll save you the trouble. There's nothing under here," she whispered. "Just me." It was soft, just a whisper of contact, but it lit him up from the inside like she'd flipped a switch he hadn't realized was off.

He groaned softly and started to lean in again, to kiss her for real, but someone tapped his shoulder.

Of course.

"Sorry to interrupt, Abe," said a guy in a velvet jacket and with a mouth full of extremely white teeth. Abe thought his name was Charles or Charlie? "You've got to come say hi to the execs from Silver Coast. They've been asking for you all night."

Abe clenched his jaw but forced a smile. "Sure. Lead the way."

He took Dylan's hand, and they were pulled back into the swirl of partygoers, moving from one circle of industry people to the next. He made the rounds, shook hands, made small talk, did the whole I'm-still-a-human-even-though-I'm-famous routine.

And Dylan? She was flawless.

He introduced her to a few well-known producers, a Grammy-winning songwriter, and even a rock legend who smelled like cigars and leather and called her "darlin'" twice. Not once did she fangirl or get googly-eyed. She just smiled politely, asked smart questions, and carried herself like she'd been doing this for years.

Damn, she was good at hiding it. Either that or she really wasn't impressed.

He caught her eye during a particularly awkward conversation about music licensing. Her lips curved into a knowing smirk, and just like that, he wanted to haul her out of there, find the nearest exit, and steal her away to somewhere they could be alone.

But the night had a rhythm of its own. They drifted towards the bar, where Dylan surprised him by ordering a dirty martini, extra olives, like it was her go-to drink. It probably wasn't. But she owned it.

At one point, he watched her standing under a cluster of hanging lights, the diamonds at her throat catching the glow just right. She looked effortless. Regal, even. Like someone meant for red carpets and private jets and yet completely untouched by all of it. She wasn't performing. She was just... her.

He didn't know how the hell he'd gotten lucky enough to have her on his arm. How in the world was he going to keep her there? Would he be lucky enough for her to want to stay?

When the party began to thin out and the music shifted to a slower tempo, Abe slipped his hand into hers and quietly signaled to the driver. No long goodbyes to the host. No promises to call from the executives.

When they finally made it back into the limo, Dylan let out a long, dramatic sigh and flopped back into the seat.

"Oh my god, my face hurts from smiling," she groaned, kicking off her heels.

Abe chuckled, loosening his collar. "You were a pro."

She turned to look at him, her cheeks flushed, her hair a little tousled, and the necklace glinting against her collarbone. "I'm never doing that again without a pre-game tequila."

He laughed. "I'll make a note."

"You were amazing, by the way," she added, more softly now. "That song... Abe, it was beautiful."

He looked over at her, his throat tightening. "It was true. Every word."

The limo curved through the glowing streets of LA, city lights flickering past the windows like stars on fast-forward. She shifted closer to him and rested her head on his shoulder.

"I don't belong in this world," she said quietly. "But... I liked watching you in it."

He kissed the top of her head. "You're wrong. You belong wherever the hell you want to be."

She smiled against his shoulder, and for the first time all night, he let himself relax. Because for once, the night hadn't been about pretending.

It had been about her.

And her being there made all of it real.

"I totally fan-girled all over Dolly. I mean, it's Dolly!" she admitted.

He smiled. "You hid it well. When I first met her, I

think I mumbled a cross between hello and hi. It came out as hi-low." He shook his head and chuckled.

Dylan smiled and then shifted closer to him. "Before we were interrupted"—she wrapped her arms around him—"you mentioned something about..." She trailed her lips across his jaw and the entire world stopped.

Everything narrowed to just her. Her scent, the feel of her body pressed against his. The taste of her mouth, her soft lips. He had to have more.

"Dylan." Her name escaped his lips like a breath.

"Abe, tell me the hotel is close." She sighed.

"Not close enough." He hit the switch for the black-out glass to close between them and the driver. Then pulled her onto his lap.

His fingers slipped up under the dress and he was thankful she hadn't worn anything underneath. She arched when his fingers found her, wet and ready for him. He used his hands and mouth on her to show her what he was going to do when they reached their hotel room.

As they were making the last turn, he felt her convulse around him as she cried out his name.

God, he wanted more. Needed more.

She was like the breath he gulped in after being deprived of air.

When the limo stopped, she was back sitting beside him, her head resting on his shoulder.

Taking her hand, he led her out and across the lobby quickly, and into the private elevator. There, he kissed her until he felt as if he was going to explode with need.

The moment their suite door closed, he pinned her against the door and kissed her while his fingers returned to slide inside her. She whipped off his jacket and tie, then tugged at the buttons on his shirt.

"More," she said when his shirt hit the ground and her nails dug into his skin.

He growled as he tried to get to her fully, then hoisted up her skirt and knelt between her legs and put his mouth to her. Tasting her sweetness and playing his tongue over her clit until he felt her convulse once more. Only then did he stand up, yank his pants down, and fully embed himself deep inside her while pinning her hands high above her head. He didn't think he could control himself if she touched him again.

Twin moans echoed in the room as his mouth covered hers. When he started to move inside her, he knew that he was finally home.

Chapter Seventeen

Being back in Portland was like waking up on the side of a highway after having the best night of your life. The fog was thick and the traffic was terrible.

Kevin had agreed to meet them at her small office at noon, and it took a little over an hour to get from the airport to downtown.

This time there was no limo, just her old Subaru that had over two hundred thousand miles on it. She'd thought about trading it in, but every time she got sticker shock and backed out.

When she parked at the small shopping center, Abe leaned forward and whistled.

"Beck Investigations." He read the sign hanging over the door.

She shrugged. "It's not flashy or catchy, just..."

"You," he finished for her, making her smile.

"Yeah. We have a few minutes before Kevin should be here." She got out and unlocked the front door and then froze.

Abe must have sensed something was wrong because he pushed past her and stepped inside.

She flipped on the lights and assessed the damage.

The small office had been ransacked.

Papers were scattered across the floor like confetti. The filing cabinet drawers hung open, their contents pulled out and tossed around. Her cork-board had been ripped from the wall, and the mini fridge had been left open, its contents dripping onto the linoleum. Her desk was the worst of it. Every drawer was ripped open, and her laptop was gone, along with the battered leather notebook she used for field notes.

"Damn," Abe muttered, stepping over a stack of files. "Someone was looking for something."

Dylan's pulse throbbed in her ears as she slowly stepped inside, her shoes crunching over a broken coffee mug. She took it all in, her space violated. Her sanctuary stripped bare. The drawer where she kept the locked file folder on Kara's case was still slightly ajar, the lock twisted like it had been forced open.

"No," she breathed, rushing to it. Sure enough, the folder was gone. "They took it. Everything physical I had on Kara."

Abe knelt beside her, resting a steady hand on her back. "This wasn't random then."

Her heart ached with a mix of anger and fear. "My laptop had encrypted files... but the folder... my notes, interviews, printouts, anyone could read that. This wasn't just someone trying to scare me. They wanted to erase... everything."

A loud knock at the door startled them both.

Kevin stood outside, his hands in his hoodie pockets and a confused look on his face.

"What the hell happened?" Kevin asked, stepping inside and glancing around.

"You tell us," Dylan said. "Whoever did this appears to have only taken what I had on your sister's case."

His eyes swept the room, settling briefly on the broken drawer. "Shit. You think this is about Kara?"

Dylan nodded slowly. "Yes, seeing as it appears that they only took her files and nothing else."

Kevin's jaw clenched.

"Guess you were getting close to something," Abe said, his arms folded. "It appears you arrived just in time to answer some questions."

"Here," Dylan said, straightening a chair and pushing the pile of paperwork on the floor aside. "Sit. Talk."

Kevin glanced at him and he motioned. "We're done hiding behind half-truths. It's time you came clean with everything."

Kevin looked between them, then sat down. "I didn't tell you everything, and I didn't tell the cops, that night, a few other parts." He shook his head and looked down at his fingers. "I didn't want to until I was sure... After Kara died, I didn't disappear because I was guilty or anything. I checked myself into rehab."

Dylan nodded. "For drinking?"

Kevin gave a humorless smile. "Hard. I was a wreck. I'd been drinking too much for months, even before Kara died, but after... I couldn't cope. I needed help, and I knew I wouldn't get it if I didn't do something. So I checked myself in and went dark. I was away for almost a year. Then, I was in and out for a few more years."

Abe frowned. "You told the cops you were home that night. The night of the accident."

"I was," Kevin said. "Alone. Watching the game and

drinking myself stupid. I wasn't lying, but I wasn't... helpful either. I didn't remember most of that night until recently. I've been piecing it back together."

"Go on," Abe said, leaning on the edge of her desk, folding his arms over his chest.

"Kara... stopped by my place after dropping you off. I lived in the same townhouses, just down two units, remember?"

Dylan felt Abe tense as he nodded.

"And?" she asked, waiting.

"And she confided in me that she was thinking of leaving you. She said you'd found out that she was cheating. She told me she smoothed things out with you, but I was pissed at her for cheating," he said to Abe. "I was drunk, too drunk." He sighed. "We fought. I said things, she said things, she left angry." He closed his eyes. "Shit, the last thing I said to her was 'fuck off.'"

"Who else was she sleeping with?" Abe asked dryly.

"I don't know. She was very secretive. I knew about a week before... before that night." He shifted.

Abe wanted to ask why he hadn't told him, but he kept his mouth shut as the hurt sank in.

"How did you find out?" Dylan asked.

Kevin glanced over at her. "I saw them together."

"Then you do know who," Abe interrupted.

"No." He shook his head a few times. "They were in her parked car. I knew it wasn't you because you were in Georgia recording. We'd just talked on the phone an hour earlier."

"Where?" Dylan asked.

"Outside my place," Kevin answered.

"Why was she with someone else outside of your place?" Abe asked.

Kevin shrugged. "I didn't ask. Kara... did whatever she wanted. Always had. I tried to shield her, protect her, but she was..."

"Kara," Abe finished and went quiet.

"You lived in the same townhouses as Abe did back then?" Dylan asked.

"A few other people we knew back then lived in those places too," Kevin said, catching on. "We'd all hung out a lot and when Abe moved in, we all sort of followed." He shrugged.

"Who else?" She sat behind her desk and found a piece of paper to jot down the names as they both listed them off.

"Do either of you suspect any of them to be the driver?" she asked.

Both men were quiet.

"One," they both said at the same time.

"One person had reason to keep a relationship quiet. To make Kara stay with me until after my album released." He shifted to stand behind her and pointed at the name. "Tony. I was his first real big client."

"Abe made him who he is today," Kevin said quietly.

"What's our next move?" Kevin asked.

Dylan looked up at him. "My next move is to find proof. Yours is to head back to Pride," she said to Abe, "and feed horses and watch your friend's lighthouse." She pointed to Kevin. "Yours is to go back home or to work or whatever and stay sober."

Then she bent down and picked up a stack of papers and started cleaning up.

After Kevin left, Abe helped her clean up and then sat across from her when she pulled out her travel laptop. She was thankful for some of the backups she had on it.

"You should keep all your files on the cloud," Abe suggested.

"Can't. Privacy concerns," she mumbled as she typed up the notes from the meeting. She looked around at her now clean office and sighed loudly. "After today, though, I guess I'll look into a secure server."

"Isn't the headquarters for Internet Security out of Pride?" Abe asked.

She stilled and then laughed. "Yes, of course." She pulled out her phone and searched for Josh William's number, then dialed it.

"Good morning, Dylan. How is my favorite PI today?" Josh answered cheerfully.

"Good." She smiled and leaned back to dive into a very long conversation. By the time she hung up, her remaining laptop was fully locked down to protect what little digital data she had left.

"Why I didn't think to contact Josh when I opened for business last year is a mystery," she said when they had stopped for dinner on their way to her apartment.

"One I'm sure you will solve," he joked as he took her hand.

When had she gone from being super nervous around him to being so comfortable? Her eyes ran over his face, and she realized that instead of seeing the famous singer she'd crushed on for years, she now saw the man that she loved with every fiber of her being.

Dylan unlocked the door to her apartment and stepped aside to let Abe in first. "Home sweet postage stamp," she joked.

The small studio apartment was cozy and tidy, every inch of space put to good use. A full-sized bed was neatly made in one corner with a navy comforter and two throw pillows stacked like it was staged for a magazine shoot. A compact couch faced the mounted TV, and the kitchenette along the far wall boasted a spotless sink, a two-burner stove, and a coffee maker that probably saw more use than anything else in the place.

Abe glanced around, smiling. "It's very you."

She dropped her bag by the door and slipped off her shoes. "Meaning what?"

"Efficient. Clean. Deceptively low-key but probably hiding a hundred useful things."

She grinned. "Flattery will get you more bed space."

He chuckled and kicked off his boots. "I'll take it."

While she settled in at her desk and opened her laptop to start rebuilding some of the files lost in the break-in, Abe took a few calls in the corner, his deep voice low and professional. Something about studio sessions, album release windows, and a possible guest appearance at an awards show. She tried not to eavesdrop but caught that he mentioned postponing everything until after his commitment watching Max's place.

Hearing him talk about leaving and going back to his normal life made her stomach flutter in a way she didn't fully trust yet.

After an hour of quiet work, she finally shut her laptop and rubbed her eyes. "I can't look at another encrypted folder tonight."

"Movie?" he offered, already scrolling through options on her TV. "I vote something with no mystery, no crime, no murder."

"Rom-com?" she asked hopefully.

He gave her a mock groan. "Fine, but only if there's popcorn."

Fifteen minutes later they were curled up together on

the couch, a bowl of buttery popcorn between them, watching a predictably cheesy romantic comedy. Halfway through, she laid her head on his shoulder, and he pressed a kiss to the top of her head. She didn't remember how the movie ended, only the steady rhythm of his breathing and the warmth of his arm around her.

The next morning, sunlight slipped through the blinds and warmed her bare feet as she shuffled around the kitchen, tossing together some breakfast.

They loaded up her Subaru around mid-morning and hit the road, windows cracked to let in the fresh summer air. Dylan glanced over at him while she navigated the busy freeway and headed out of Portland. Abe's sunglasses were hiding his eyes, but his hand was warm over hers on the center console.

For the first time in her life, Pride felt far away, something she couldn't wait to be closer to.

This wasn't just a drive back to a town she'd grown up in and left because there were too many memories she wanted to avoid. This was the place she had found him. Found something she never expected. Love. And it was the start of something she wasn't ready to give up.

The sun glinted off the hood of her car as they cruised down the highway. The trees were flying by in a blur of green and gold. With Abe's hand warm on hers, it was easy to forget the reason they had met in the first place. Easy to let herself believe for just a little while that everything was simple. She was a girl who had fallen for a man.

But of course, it wasn't.

She adjusted the rearview mirror, more out of habit than necessity, and glanced sideways at him. "There's something that keeps bothering me about the night Kara died," she said, her voice quieter than she'd intended.

Abe looked over at her, his sunglasses still shielding his eyes. "What?"

"We've cleared Kevin from our list, basically. But I keep coming back to one thing that doesn't sit well."

He shifted in his seat, alert now. "Was it really Tony Carson behind the wheel?"

She nodded slowly. "Yeah."

"If so, how did we not know?" he asked.

She shook her head slowly. "Did he do it on purpose? The marks on her were done before she died. If it was him, then..." She glanced over at him. "That means he killed her."

Abe took a deep breath and leaned his head back on the headrest.

The silence stretched between them for a few miles, broken only by the hum of the tires on the asphalt and the occasional bird overhead.

"I haven't found anything concrete yet," she admitted, "tying Tony to Kara. A lot of your friends from back then lived in those townhomes. There isn't one text message or phone call from his known numbers to hers."

"Tony seems the most logical at this point. He had the most to gain from my career taking off. He and Kara used to be really close, before we started dating. So it seems reasonable."

She gave a slow, deliberate nod. "He was just a few units over from Kevin's place."

"That doesn't mean anything," Abe said, but his voice had lost some of its certainty. "Without proof."

"I know. Believe me, I'm looking everywhere for something," Dylan said. "But the timing and location adds up. I did some digging before we left. According to one police report, Kara had been seen coming and going from that complex more than once."

Abe ran a hand over his face. "He was dating a singer that he was managing. A woman whose career took a nose dive a few months later."

"Elena Vale," Dylan filled in for him. "She was supposed to be America's next pop princess, and she was his very public girlfriend at the time of Kara's death. If it ever came out that he was having an affair with a college student who was dating his best friend, not to mention that she died the night they were together? His whole world would've gone up in flames."

"I still can't wrap my head around that," Abe muttered, staring out the window. "He used to bring Kara coffee when he came over. He used to say that she reminded him of his little sister."

Dylan arched a brow. "Do you call your sister at midnight for a hookup? The call logs of that mysterious number all show they talked more than you and she did."

"Point taken." He sighed.

She adjusted her grip on the wheel. "The part that drives me crazy is how clean the whole thing is. The car was Kara's, the keys were in the ignition, and Kevin admits to drinking that night and blacking out. He could have been an easy scapegoat. If Tony wanted to frame anyone, he was the easy target. Not you." She hesitated.

Abe let out a long breath. "You really think Tony was the one behind the wheel?"

"I think he could have been," she said carefully. "But I have no proof. No witnesses. No camera footage. Nothing that would hold up in court."

He was quiet for a beat. "And if it was him? That means

Kara lied to me that night. About everything. That Tony has been lying to me for years."

She reached over and squeezed his hand. "Or she didn't. Maybe she didn't even know who she wanted. Maybe she was confused, caught between two lives. You said she encouraged your music career, right? Maybe that was her trying to do the right thing?"

He gave her a sad half-smile as she turned off the main highway and started towards the winding road that would take them back to Pride. "You're good at giving people the benefit of the doubt."

"I try." Her voice cracked a little. "But I'm also a realist and a PI. I have seen the dark side of people. If Tony was the one behind the wheel, it explains a lot. Why there were no charges against you, why the investigation dried up. Why the reports went quiet. Why the PR machine around Kara's death spun out so fast it made her family dizzy and angry. He would've had the reach, the connections... to make the story dry up."

Abe leaned his head back against the seat and closed his eyes. "Jesus."

They drove in silence for a while, both lost in their thoughts. The trees grew taller and denser as they neared the outskirts of Pride. The air smelled sweeter here, like cedar and possibility.

Finally, Dylan spoke again, softly. "I'll keep digging. I'll find out what really happened."

Suddenly the car jerked forward with a loud bang as metal clashed on metal. Her head banged against the side of her door.

She heard screaming, felt her skin break open, cut by the shards of glass and debris that flew towards her hands and face. There was a rapid sensation of burning and a puff of smoke as the airbag exploded in her face.

She grunted when the steering wheel was shoved into her chest. Her left knee collided with the door and was smashed against the steering column.

The world tilted, twisted, turned, and finally, before any of the pain could set in, stilled.

She blinked a few times, confused.

"Dylan!" she heard Abe shouting over the ringing in her ears.

She turned to look towards him, but before she could say his name, the car was hit again. Once more the scenery outside spun. She could see the blue sky. Green grass and trees. Then rocks and ocean. She screamed again just before everything went dark.

Chapter Eighteen

Pain. The sound of waves.
Pain. The smell of salt water.
Pain. Pain. Pain.

With each wave that crashed onto the rocks, there was a pulse of pain that exploded everywhere. It consumed every single inch of his body.

What?

Where?

Why?

Dylan!

His eyes flew open. Desperate. Searching.

His throat was raw as he cried out for her.

His hands cut on rocks, glass, metal, as he searched.

His clothes were soaked. His right knee wouldn't work, so he crawled across rocks towards the metal ball that used to be her car.

How had he gotten out of it? Why was he on the beach?

Then, a memory flashed quickly of him removing his seatbelt after the initial accident. He'd reached over for her, to help her, then... they had fallen off a cliff.

He spared a quick glance up, twenty maybe thirty feet up, where the road was. He continued to crawl through sand, rocks, debris. To her.

"Dylan," he cried when he finally reached the car.

She was there, hanging upside down, her arms falling straight down, her hands resting on the top of her car. Her eyes were closed. Tiny cuts covered her face, arms, and hands.

"Dylan," he said, sitting beside the car.

Her phone was right there, by her hand. Without thinking, he reached for it and punched 911 on its shattered screen. While he relayed their location, he felt for a pulse on Dylan's neck with shaky hands. Feeling a strong beat, he let out a sigh of relief.

From what he could tell, she was whole. Cut up, bruised, maybe more, but she was alive.

He didn't dare move her. First off, he doubted that he could catch her if he removed her seatbelt, which would cause her to fall head-first into the top of her twisted up car. Second, his vision was slowly fading, which meant he was most likely going to pass out soon.

He didn't know how long he waited, biting the inside of his lip to keep himself awake. When he heard the sirens and the helicopter, he leaned back against the car door and held onto Dylan's hand, feeling her steady heartbeat and waiting for rescue.

He woke as he was wheeled down a long bright hallway and instantly closed his eyes as pain shot through his head.

"Abe?" someone called to him. His eyes flew open when he realized it was Dylan. She was there, hovering above him, holding his hand. She had fresh bandages on her face and dark bruises under each eye, as if her nose had been broken. She was wearing a different shirt, maybe a hospital gown. She looked tired and the most beautiful she'd ever looked before.

"Dylan," he groaned. "Are you hurt?"

She shook her head and a tear slipped down her face. "No, I'm okay. Cuts, bruises." She smiled at him.

"Am I hurt?" he asked, feeling numbness. Her smile slipped. "My knee?"

She nodded slowly. "They're going to prep you for surgery. They said something about pins." She shook her head and wiped her eyes. "You were out for so long, I... I made the call and okayed the surgery."

"I trust you." He sighed. "When?"

"Now, they're wheeling you back now. I'll—" She was interrupted by a person in scrubs.

"Sorry, you can't go any further."

"I love you," she said quickly, then leaned down and placed her lips over his. "I'll see you when you get out."

"Okay." He tried to reach for her but his hands were locked down. "Dylan," he called as he started moving again.

"Yeah?" she said from somewhere behind him.

"I love you, too."

He heard her sob as the doors behind him shut, then he slipped back into darkness.

The next time he woke it was dark, quiet, and a warm hand was holding his.

"Dylan?" he said, his voice nothing more than a croak.

"I'm here," she said, and he heard her shift closer as a low light turned on.

Just seeing her face had him smiling. "How'd I do?" he asked.

She nodded with a smile. "Pins are in. They say it will be a few months before you're back on a horse."

He smiled. "You?"

"Good. Like I said, cuts, bruises." She shrugged. "Banged up knee, but not as bad as yours, and a slight concussion. My car is sitting on the beach about thirty feet below the road." She glanced to her side, then back at him. "The police think that someone pushed us over the edge on purpose. I told them about my office being broken into."

"Who?" he frowned. "Tony?"

"They're checking into where he was." She rested her forehead on their joined hands.

"You told me that you love me," he reminded her.

Her head popped up and she smiled. "And you said it back."

"Are we going to talk about it?" He lifted her hand to his lips and brushed a kiss across her knuckles, avoiding the bandages and bruises.

"Do we have to?" She smiled down at him.

He thought about it and nodded slowly. "I have never told anyone that before," he admitted. "Not even Kara. You?"

She shook her head. "My dad." She shrugged.

"Okay, I stand corrected, I told my mom all the time. This is different." She nodded. "I love you. I don't want this to be awkward."

"It's not." She leaned up to brush her lips across his. "First things first. If Tony just tried to kill us, I'd like to not be worried that he'll try again when he finds out he failed."

"Ditto. Plus, there's this whole..." He motioned to his leg. "I guess I should ask what else on me is busted, since most of me is numb."

"Cuts, bruises." She stretched her shoulders. "They said they found you outside the car. Did you crawl around?"

"I took my seatbelt off after the first crash. I guess I fell out when the car was pushed over the edge. I landed in the soft part of the sand."

Her eyes went wide. "You could have..." Her face paled slightly as she thought about the possibilities. Yeah, he was doing the same. He could have landed in the water or, worse, on the rocks.

"Hey," he said, distracting her, "let's put that away for now too." She nodded. "Did you get some sleep?"

She shook her head. "I couldn't, until I knew you were okay."

He motioned to the other side of the bed, where there was more space, away from his bad knee. "Climb up here." He shifted as she crawled up gently next to him. When she laid her head on his shoulder, he held in a groan and winced.

Okay, more than just the knee was hurt.

"Are you okay?" she asked.

"Yeah," he lied and shifted again until the pain disappeared. "Rest," he said. He drifted off listening to the sound of her breathing.

The following morning, after he'd downed the breakfast that had been delivered, he and Dylan talked to Aiden Brogan and Tom Reyes, Pride's local police, who were investigating the crash.

"Tony Carson was in LA last night at the premiere of one of his client's movies," Aiden said, looking at his notes. "There are pictures and videos of him there all throughout the night."

He saw Dylan's shoulders sink. "Okay, if it wasn't him, then..." She turned towards him.

"What are the chances it was just an accident?" Abe asked.

"If they would have left your car on the road, a high

chance, but the tire marks show that they purposely pushed you off the cliff. Right through the guardrail," Tom answered. "The two of you are very lucky. Not a lot of people would have survived a thirty-foot drop. The mechanic said it was thanks to the older car. Some of those things are built like tanks."

"I've never been so glad that I didn't trade her in," Dylan whispered.

"Any idea on the vehicle that hit us? The make, model?" he asked the officers.

"We're working on it. We'll let you know when we find out something ourselves. They told us that you'll be in here for about a week," Aiden said. He handed Dylan a card. "My cell phone number is on the back. Technically, you're currently in Edgeview's jurisdiction until you return to Pride, but if you need anything..." He nodded to the card. "Night or day."

"Thanks." Dylan slid the card into the pocket of her jeans, which Lucy had delivered earlier that morning. Apparently, her old friend had sat with her the entire time he was in surgery and had promised to bring her fresh clothes in the morning.

After Dylan had showered that morning, Lucy had shown up with a bag of clothes, and they had gone down to the cafeteria and had coffee and chatted while he ate his breakfast.

After the two officers left, she sat next to him on the bed and they watched television.

He was slightly surprised when a report on their accident appeared on the news. An overhead video of Dylan's car lying upside down on the rocky beach flashed on the screen.

"Oh my god," she said, sitting up slightly. "How did we

make it?" The image shifted, like it had been taken from a drone or a helicopter.

He took her hand in his and squeezed lightly. "Luck."

She glanced at him. "I don't know if I'll ever be able to drive that stretch of road again."

"You will." He smiled. "After we catch the bastard that did this to us."

She nodded. "My laptop was destroyed, but I uploaded all my data last night to my new secure server." She smiled. "Josh has promised to drop off a new laptop here to me today. Then we can start from scratch. If it wasn't Tony, who else lived in those townhouses?"

He tried to think, but thanks to the full meal and the pain meds, his head was numb.

"I'm too tired to think," he admitted after trying to remember anything from all those years ago.

"Sleep." She planted a kiss on his lips. "I'll be right here."

"Who's taking care of the horses?" he asked groggily.

"I called Nate. He's staying there watching over the house and the horses until they release you. Rest. Everything is taken care of."

"I love you," he said, and he drifted off.

Chapter Nineteen

"Easy," Dylan warned as Nate helped Abe up the stairs.

"Yes, Mom," Nate teased as he shifted to take a little more of Abe's weight.

"I could have done this myself," Abe complained while Nate practically carried him through the front door.

"No, you couldn't. You're not allowed to put any weight on that leg until you see the doctor in two weeks," she warned. "And it is my mission to keep you off your feet."

"Sounds like heaven," Nate joked. He nudged Abe, practically sending him falling just inside the door. "Sorry," he mumbled. He caught Abe and helped him over to the sofa.

"I'll go check on Stormy and Blaze." Nate quickly disappeared.

Once Nate was out the door, Dylan knelt beside the couch, adjusting the pillows behind Abe and tucking a blanket over his lap. The cozy place was quiet again, the kind of quiet she hadn't experienced in days.

Abe leaned his head back against the cushion and sighed. "I missed this couch."

She smiled and brushed a lock of hair off his forehead. "You missed the view. Admit it."

His lips curved. "Depends. Do you mean the one outside or the one currently bossing me around?"

She stood with a small laugh. "Flattery won't get you pie."

He groaned dramatically. "There's pie?"

"There will be. After lunch. A bunch of townspeople showed up and dropped off food for you."

"For us, you mean. You went off that cliff too, and you're staying here to watch over me."

"Rest." She leaned over and kissed him. "You look worn out."

While he rested on the sofa watching television, she headed into the kitchen to heat up some of the meals that had been dropped off for them. The freezer was full of things, all labeled with their ingredients and instructions for heating them up.

A while later, the kitchen smelled of rosemary and roasted garlic. Every so often she glanced at Abe, who was flipping through the TV with the sound low, his crutches leaning against the arm of the couch, his leg propped up on two pillows.

Even though it had only been a week since the accident, it felt like a lifetime. The screech of metal, the gut-lurching drop, the rocks slamming against the car as they tumbled towards the beach—all of it still haunted her dreams.

She plated their lunch and brought it to the coffee table, handing Abe his before curling up beside him with her own. "No complaints about not having to cook for a while," she said with a laugh.

"I'm on painkillers. You could've handed me cardboard, and I'd be grateful," he murmured, eyeing the pasta hungrily.

They ate in silence for a while, the familiar comfort wrapping around them like a blanket. Outside, the sky had started to darken, thick clouds rolling in from the west, bruising the horizon.

Once he was done eating, she took their plates into the kitchen and washed them. Then she brought out the cherry pie and ice cream.

While they ate their sweets, he turned the station to one of the late night shows and they laughed together at the jokes.

By the time the show was over, he was fast asleep on the sofa.

She retrieved her new laptop from their shared room and took it back out to the living room. She sat across from him and worked until she too drifted off for a quick nap.

She was still bruised in places, but most of her small cuts had healed already. Her knee was still sore where it hit the car door, but other than that, she was thankfully almost back to normal.

Later that evening, just as she was heating them up some dinner, the storm arrived.

Thunder cracked over the water, and the windows shook in their frames. Dylan stood at the back door, watching lightning streak across the sky as rain pelted the roof. The horses were secured in the barn, and Nate had texted earlier saying that he'd gone home to change and would be back first thing in the morning to check on them again.

She turned to find Abe half-asleep again on the couch, his leg propped up and the blanket tucked snugly around him. She reached for a candle and lit it, just in case the power blinked out.

Lightning flashed and less than a second later, a boom of thunder made her flinch as it rattled the dishes in the cupboards.

"Okay," she whispered, as the lights flickered once and went dark. The light from the television went out, sending the entire house into darkness.

Now, the only light was the candle she held in her shaky hands.

"No ghosts. No murderers. Just a storm," she told herself softly.

She double-checked the front door, then moved to the kitchen to check the back door. That's when she heard it.

The sound of a floorboard creaking somewhere from inside the large house.

She froze.

The breath she'd just taken was frozen in her lungs.

It hadn't come from the kitchen or the TV, since it was still off, along with everything else in the massive house.

Seconds ticked by and she heard the generator kick on outside for the lighthouse. The bright light swung around outside the windows, temporarily lighting portions of the rooms.

Shadows played over spaces, making everything ominous.

Had the noise come from somewhere deeper in the house. Had it been her imagination?

Her heartbeat thundered louder than the storm as she reached slowly into the drawer, closing her hand around the handle of the heavy flashlight that she had seen in there when she was looking for a can opener.

It wasn't her gun, which was tucked in her purse back in

the room she would be sharing with Abe, along with her cell phone. In a pinch, the heavy flashlight would have to do.

She heard another floor board creaking and glanced to where Abe was still fast asleep. She knew that his pain meds would keep him out for hours at a time. Since he'd taken them shortly after lunch, he would be out for at least another hour.

She doubted there was time to creep down the hallway and get her gun or her cell phone. His phone had been lost in the accident and they hadn't replaced it yet.

Fear had her heading towards the living room, where Abe was.

Another sound. This one louder. A creak of wood. A deliberate step.

Someone really was inside the house.

Lightning flashed, illuminating the hallway.

For a second, just a second, she thought she saw an outline of a person, but no, it couldn't be. A man in a sailor's outfit. The shadows were playing tricks on her.

Then another flash and she saw a different shadow retreating around the corner near the bedrooms.

She turned off the flashlight, relying on the storm's intermittent flashes and the lighthouse's bright light to guide her.

The air felt electric. Charged.

She crept forward, heart pounding in her throat. She purposely put herself between the sounds and Abe, willing to risk everything to protect the man she loved. Behind her, Abe stirred.

"Dylan?" His voice was groggy.

She turned just enough to whisper, "Stay there. Someone's here."

That sobered him instantly.

She heard the rustle of the blanket, the soft thump as he reached for his crutches, but she shook her head fiercely. "Don't move," she hissed.

There was a crash from the back of the house as something fell or was knocked over. Then silence.

Pure, aching silence.

Dylan's skin prickled. She took another step towards the hallway, flashlight raised.

And then nothing.

No one appeared. No more sounds came.

The storm raged louder, rattling the glass, as Dylan slowly took a step closer.

She felt Abe half standing, half leaning on the chair next to her.

"Are you sure?" he whispered.

"Yeah." She nodded just as the shadow appeared in the doorway.

"You should have left it alone," a voice said. "No one cared what happened to that slut all those years ago."

Abe gasped as Reba Lyle stepped out of the shadows, dressed in all black, holding Dylan's gun in gloved hands.

"Reba?" Abe's voice was shallow, as if he couldn't believe his eyes.

"I never meant for you to get hurt," Reba said to him. "Just her." She motioned and pointed the gun at Dylan. "She was the one poking around. The one who was going to expose everything."

Suddenly, everything fell into place for Dylan. All those loose pieces suddenly clicked. Every unanswered question made sense.

"James was having an affair with Kara, your best friend. He was the one driving that night. The night Kara died," she said, certain.

Reba's eyes shifted between them.

"I... I knew for a while about them. He kept promising he was going to stop seeing her. That after your record went big, he'd make you break things off with her and we would never have to see that slut again." She swayed slightly.

Was the woman drunk again? Was that the reason she drank? Guilt? Remorse? Fear of being discovered?

"When James came home that night, he was covered in blood. He told me about the accident. Confessed that he'd been drinking. So I went there, to the accident, hoping..." She shook her head. "But Kara was awake. Trapped in the wreckage. She was begging me to help her."

"She was alive?" Abe gasped and leaned more on the chair.

"What did you do?" Dylan asked, trying to think of possible ways to escape what was going to happen next.

"I warned her to stay away from my husband, but she was determined. She told me that he was leaving me. She laughed about how they had just made love and that they had been heading back to the townhouse to tell me and you that they were in love and going to run off together," Reba said, her voice rising slightly. "We were trying to start our family." She screamed the last.

"What did you do?" Dylan asked again, knowing she needed to stall long enough to come up with a plan. So far, all she could think of was to throw the flashlight at the woman's head and run, but that would leave Abe to fend for himself, something she would never do.

"I picked up a rock and hit her until she stopped screaming. It wasn't hard. She was trapped in the wreckage. Her legs were pinned and one of her feet was at an angle. She probably would have bled out sooner or later." She smiled. "The bitch deserved it."

"You? You ran us off the road and pushed us over the cliff?" Abe asked.

Reba's eyes moved to him. She opened her mouth to answer and that is when Dylan saw her opening.

Instead of throwing the flashlight at the woman, she threw her entire body. They hit the wall, bounced off it, and then she flipped the smaller woman over like a rag doll.

The gun flew out of her hands, landing somewhere in the darkness as she used all the years of training to hold down the smaller woman, pinning her to the floor.

"Can you get my phone?" she asked Abe, holding onto Reba as she tried to fight her. Honestly, she was no match for Dylan's skill. "It's in my purse in our bedroom. Crawl if you have to."

"I think I can. Are you okay?" he asked as he hobbled by them.

Reba was crying and screaming nonsense as Dylan gripped her arms hard behind her back, pushing her knee between the woman's shoulder blades.

"Yeah, she's a lightweight," she said, not willing to take her eyes off Reba. "Call 911 or Aiden. His number is programmed in my phone," she called out as she heard Abe make his way slowly down the hallway.

"You fucked up," she whispered into Reba's ear.

"You'll ruin everything," she screamed. "James will lose everything. It will destroy Abe. All because of that slut!"

"No." She smiled and jerked her arms a little harder. "You just cleared Abe's name. The only one who is ruined is you." She smiled. "You killed your best friend out of jealousy. You've destroyed your husband's career, exposing his lies. He covered for you for all these years. He'll pay. Just like you will."

Reba bucked and tried to break free. Dylan sat on her, using all her weight.

"You bitch! You've ruined everything. Do you really think someone like Abe could ever love you?" Reba hissed.

At that moment, Abe came back into the room, talking on the phone with Aiden.

Dylan smiled and locked eyes with him.

"Yes. Yes, I do believe someone like Abe could love someone like me."

Abe smiled and, suddenly, nothing else in the world mattered.

Epilogue

The bright lights almost blinded her, and she swayed slightly.

"Easy," Abe said from behind her. "I've got you."

She smiled over at him and wrapped her arms around his waist. "Yes, you do."

He chuckled and then planted a kiss on her. "So, do you know how all this works?"

She glanced around and nodded. "You go out there, play a bunch of songs and have all those women dream about you, then you take me home and I get to have you."

He laughed again. "Something like that." He kissed her again just as he was introduced.

"Break a leg," she said, thinking that he'd drop his hold on her and walk out onto the stage to thousands of screaming fans. Instead, he wrapped his fingers around hers and pulled her out onto the stage with him. In his left hand he held a microphone, and he spoke into it as they entered the spotlight.

"Good evening, LA," he called out and had the entire stadium cheering.

It was deafening. Her heart skipped. Her entire body tensed.

She'd never stood in front of so many people in her life. Never cared to.

He stopped in the middle of the stage.

"Many of you might have heard that last year I was in a little... accident." He glanced over at her. The audience booed and then clapped. Someone shouted, "We love you, Abe!" from the front row.

"I love you too." He winked and cheers erupted again.

"Well, I'm here tonight, on my first tour since then, with a very special someone." He held up their joined hands and the crowd went wild. When the cheering died down a little, he turned towards her. The entire stadium gasped when he went down on his knee, his good knee, still holding her hand in his. "Dylan Beck, we've been through a lot together—flying off cliffs, having guns pointed at us, moving homes, remodeling, buying horses together." He smiled.

"Get on with it," someone shouted from the front row.

Dylan glanced over and saw Nate smiling up at them and laughed.

"Shut up, Nate," Abe said with a chuckle. Then he turned his gaze back to her. "What I'm trying, but failing, to say is, will you marry me?"

She smiled and knelt beside him. As she cupped his face in her hands, the entire world faded away until all she could see was him.

"I've loved you from the moment you swaggered onto the beach during that bonfire," she said softly. "I'll love you until our end. Yes." She laughed when the stadium erupted again. "I'll marry you," she finished as her lips pressed against his.

Also by Jill Sanders

The Pride Series
Finding Pride

Discovering Pride

Returning Pride

Lasting Pride

Serving Pride

Red Hot Christmas

My Sweet Valentine

Return To Me

Rescue Me

A Pride Christmas

The Secret Series
Secret Seduction

Secret Pleasure

Secret Guardian

Secret Passions

Secret Identity

Secret Sauce

Secret Obsession

Secret Desire

Secret Charm

Secret Santa

The West Series

Loving Lauren

Taming Alex

Holding Haley

Missy's Moment

Breaking Travis

Roping Ryan

Wild Bride

Corey's Catch

Tessa's Turn

Saving Trace

Christmas Holly

Maggie's Match

The Grayton Series

Last Resort

Someday Beach

Rip Current

In Too Deep

Swept Away

High Tide

Sunset Dreams

Lucky Series

Unlucky In Love

Sweet Resolve

Best of Luck

A Little Luck

Christmas Wish

Silver Cove Series

Silver Lining

French Kiss

Happy Accident

Hidden Charm

A Silver Cove Christmas

Sweet Surrender

Second Chances

Dancing on Air

Entangled Series – Paranormal Romance

The Awakening

The Beckoning

The Ascension

The Presence

The Calling

The Chosen

The Beyond

The Void

The Stars

The Goddess

Haven, Montana Series

Closer to You

Never Let Go

Holding On
Coming Home
The Hard Way
Never Again

Pride Oregon Series

A Dash of Love
My Kind of Love
Season of Love
Tis the Season
Dare to Love
Where I Belong
Because of Love
A Thing Called Love
First Comes Love
Someone to Love
Fools in Love
FindingLove
Christmas Joy
Always My Love
Forever My Love
Searching for Love
Love Like Ours
Wrtiten With Love
Art of Love
Unspoken Love

Wildflowers Series

Summer Nights

Summer Heat

Summer Secrets

Summer Fling

Summer's End

Summer Wish

Summer Breeze

Summer Ride

Summer Affair

Summer Ever After

Distracted Series

Wake Me

Tame Me

Save Me

Dare Me

Stand Alone Books

Twisted Rock

Hope Harbor

Raven Falls

Angel Bluff

Day Break

Diamonds in the Mud

For a complete list of books:

http://JillSanders.com

About the Author

Jill Sanders is a New York Times, USA Today, and international bestselling author of Sweet Contemporary Romance, Romantic Suspense, Western Romance, and Paranormal Romance novels. With over 100 books in eleven series, translations into several different languages, and audiobooks there's plenty to choose from. Look for Jill's bestselling stories wherever romance books are sold or visit her at jillsanders.com

Jill comes from a large family with six siblings, including an identical twin. She was raised in the Pacific Northwest and later relocated to Colorado for college and a successful IT career before discovering her talent for writing sweet and sexy page-turners. After Colorado, she decided to move south, living in Texas and now making her home along the Emerald Coast of Florida. You will find that the settings of several of her series are inspired by her time spent living in these areas. She has two sons and off-set the testosterone in her house by adopting three furry little ladies that provide her company while she's locked in her writing cave. She enjoys heading to the beach, hiking, swimming, wine-tasting, and pickleball with her husband, and of course writing. If you have read any of her books, you may also notice that there is a love of food, especially sweets! She has been blamed for a few added pounds by her assistant, editor, and fans... donuts or pie anyone?

- facebook.com/JillSandersBooks
- x.com/JillMSanders
- amazon.com/Jill-Sanders/e/B009M2NFD6?tag=jillm-com-20
- bookbub.com/authors/jill-sanders
- instagram.com/jillsandersauthor
- tiktok.com/@jillsandersauthor

www.ingramcontent.com/pod-product-compliance
Lightning Source LLC
LaVergne TN
LVHW041804060526
838201LV00046B/1124